JUST A LUCKY BREAK-IN

A LUCY FONG MYSTERY

ANNE R. TAN

1

AN OCEAN BREEZE

"Hi, Mom. It's Lucy. If you can hear me, please move your fingers."

Lucy Fong held her breath, waiting for her mother's lifeless hand to twitch. The clock on the wall of the hospital room ticked. The machine hooked up to her mother's body whirled and dripped nourishment and medication, but her mother's hand remained still as the grave.

She closed her eyes and bowed her head, praying to her Chinese ancestors. Though her mother wasn't Chinese, surely her father's side of the family wouldn't begrudge helping someone who meant the world to Lucy.

A tear leaked down her face. She hadn't spoken to her mother in the last sixteen years, and now that she was ready to give their relationship another chance, her mother wasn't available.

Lucy's bitter smile wobbled. Unavailable. Like her mother was off doing something else. Lucy refused to give in to the fear that, this time, it might be too late. Whoever shot her mother was behind bars and awaiting trial, but it didn't make waiting for her mom to wake up from a coma any easier.

In Lucy's memory, Mom was a tall and willowy woman with blonde hair and a vibrant personality to match it. She was the polar opposite of Lucy, who had been a serious and reserved child. But that was a lifetime ago. The elderly woman in the hospital bed had a permanent frown on her face. The thinning white hair spread around her like a shroud.

The fluorescent lights overhead cast a gray pallor over the hospital room despite the cheerful yellow painted walls. The room was barely big enough to fit the hospital bed, the medical equipment, and the chair. On one wall, there was a tall narrow window like the kind found in a medieval castle. Maybe the hospital board was afraid the patient would jump from the second-floor room. Next to the window was a door that led to a bathroom, which no one had used since her comatose mother had occupied the room.

Footsteps approached her mother's room. The whispered conversation drifted in and out, adding to the otherworldly feeling of life being on hold in an extended hospital stay. It took a few minutes for Lucy to realize she recognized the voices in the conversation. It was her mother's cousin, Estelle Faye—who went by Stella since her makeover—and Nurse Bobbi.

Lucy frowned. What were the two of them talking about? She strained her ears and concentrated on their voices.

"...physical therapy...at least three months...maybe longer."

"...side...in-home checkup..."

"I don't think...Lucy..."

At Nurse Bobbi's mention of her name, Lucy's attention perked up. Now she was sure that Stella was up to something. However, since Lucy was the next of kin, the doctor wouldn't make a decision about her mother's care without at least consulting her. So whatever Stella was up to, it had nothing to do with Mom.

Lucy got up from the chair next to her mother's bedside and tiptoed to the door. She waited for several seconds but couldn't hear anything. She took a step into the hallway, just as Stella came into the room. For an awkward second, the two of them tried to shift out of the way at the same time, and Lucy ended up ramming into Stella's armpit. When they finally stopped moving, Lucy sidestepped, and Stella came into the room.

Like all the women on the Faye side of the family, Stella Faye was tall, towering over Lucy even without heels. Before her miraculous makeover with Lucy's foster grandma, Stella had teeth and ears that seemed too big for her face. Her long blonde hair had hung heavy and limp, dragging down her features rather than highlighting them. Even though she was in her early fifties, she had looked like someone much older. In one afternoon and a few hundred dollars later, Stella blossomed into a bombshell.

She had chopped off her long hair, opting for a pixie cut like Lucy's, but instead of red streaks, Stella put in warm highlights, which softened the contrast with her facial features. With more movement to her hair, she was able to hide her ears. The skillful application of pale pink lipstick gave her lips more volume, making the teeth appear smaller. Stella looked a decade younger and more like Lucy's older sister.

Unlike her mother's cousin, Lucy felt like she had aged a decade in the few weeks since her return to Morro Cliff. Maybe it was the stress of her mother's condition or helping her younger half-sister move out of town, but Lucy had put on weight. She always had more padding than the other women in the family, thanks to her Chinese father. She was also shorter, darker, and overall hairier like Cousin Itt from *The Adams Family* movie.

Stella peered at Mom's face. "Any changes today?"

Lucy shook her head. "I'm beginning to lose hope."

"Never lose hope, my dear. Miracles happen every day. I've seen it in my line of work."

Stella was a former pharmacist who was forced into an early retirement a year ago. During her career, she must have seen patients making lifestyle changes that reversed their ailments. Though how Mom could make lifestyle changes in her current state was beyond Lucy's comprehension.

"Were you talking to Nurse Bobbi out in the hallway?" Lucy asked. "Was it about Mom?"

Stella fiddled with the blanket, tucking it around Mom, even though the patient couldn't move to disturb the bedding. "The nurse and I were talking about what Dahlia might need to recover her strength."

Lucy blinked. Wasn't it too early to discuss physical therapy when Mom hadn't even woken up yet? "I didn't know you were such an optimist. I can only get through one day at a time."

Stella shrugged awkwardly. "I've been a caregiver my entire life, so that's the first thing I think about."

She had returned home after college to take care of her aging parents. She glanced at the clock on the wall. "What time is the locksmith showing up at the shop?"

Lucy grabbed her purse. "In twenty minutes. Are you coming?"

Stella made a shooing motion with her hands. "We don't need two people to watch the locksmith drill out a lock. Let me sit with Dahlia for a few minutes. But I'll be there before the meeting with the mayor."

As Lucy strolled past the nurse's station, she felt harried like she had missed the ball. The meeting with the mayor would determine if she could lease out the vacant retail space in her mother's shopping plaza. The rents from the yarn shop and the newspaper office paid for the mortgage Mom took out for her sister's college tuition. Without another source of income, the hospital bills would drain Mom's entire savings well before she woke up.

As the temporary head of the family, it was Lucy's responsibility to make sure this didn't happen. Stella was the public figurehead for the family private investigation office—she was the only one licensed by the state—but she was already retired. In addition, Stella's branch of the family wasn't in the direct line of succession for the Faye

Family Trust. Mom had inherited the private investigation office, and Lucy was next in line.

While Lucy might be estranged from her mother, she understood filial piety—thanks to the Chinese uncle who took her in as a runaway teen. She figured this was the universe balancing everything out. Now it was her turn to take care of someone else.

LUCY FELT SLIGHTLY SILLY, watching the locksmith drill out the lock of the vacant shop. He didn't need her hovering while he worked, but if she went inside the PI office, he might have questions for her. So here she stood, twiddling her thumbs.

From the corner of Lucy's eye, she could see Damien North studying her from inside the newspaper office. The man stood in front of the shop's glass windows with a mug in his hand. It wouldn't take more than a glance to get Damien to come out.

Tall, dark, and slightly mysterious—and according to Stella, Damien was every woman's dream. He was in his early forties with black hair and warm brown eyes. At five feet eleven, he had a lean runner's physique. At one point in his family tree, someone married a Hispanic, and Damien had inherited the Hispanic skin tone.

He did odd jobs for his rich uncle and running the newspaper was one of them. His uncle was as eccentric as Lucy's foster grandma but without the common sense. Not only did Damien have a nosy streak, but he had also hinted at kicking their friendship up a notch. Too bad Lucy wasn't interested.

She was here to get Mom back on her feet, not to indulge in a temporary romantic liaison. And besides, if he was such a catch, how come a woman hadn't snatched him up by now? Ergo, there must be something wrong with the man.

Lucy turned her back and glanced inside the windows of the yarn shop. The Vietnamese shop owner appeared to be in the middle of a class in the back corner. Good. She was equally as curious as Damien and also wanted to kick their acquaintance up to the BFF level.

In a different circumstance, Lucy would find all this attention flattering, but her first priority was her family. She didn't have any spare emotional energy for anyone else.

The locksmith pulled out a small drill from his tool bag. "Looks like I'll have to drill it out and put in a new one."

"Okay. Do whatever you need," Lucy said because she felt like he needed a reply.

Her cell phone rang, and she pulled it out of her purse. It was from Stella. She turned her back to the locksmith and tapped on the screen to accept the incoming call.

"What's up? Did Mom wake up?" Lucy's pulse jumped at the thought.

"No. I'm calling to let you know the mayor is on his way," Stella said.

Lucy frowned. She was supposed to have an hour to replace the lock and look around the vacant shop. They didn't know if the last tenant left the place in good condition. "We still haven't opened the door yet. Can you stall him?"

"I can try, but I probably can't buy you more than ten or fifteen minutes."

"I thought he had the hots for you. Can't you flirt with him for a bit? Bat your eyes?"

"Um, no, thanks. I don't have flings with married men."

They said their goodbyes and hung up.

The hair on the back of Lucy's neck stiffened. She glanced up to see Damien North inside her personal space, drinking from his mug and watching the locksmith. She had no idea how long he had been standing here or how much of the phone call he had heard. She took a side step to give herself more space.

"Do you smell that?" Damien whispered from the side of his mouth, leaning toward her as if they had been having an intimate conversation all along.

Lucy had to give the man credit for being persistent. She glanced at the locksmith. Sweat stains from his armpits soaked his company polo shirt. "It's hard to perform under all this attention."

"I don't think it's him. Maybe a skunk?" Damien whispered.

Lucy breathed in cautiously. Her nose twitched at the rancid and fetid scent. "I hope not. Skunk oil can linger for days. Let's hope the ocean breeze can blow away the smell."

"So, the mayor wants to rent this place for the town museum, huh?" Damien said.

Lucy groaned inwardly. Sometimes she couldn't tell where his professional curiosity ended, and their friendship began. Since nothing was final yet, she didn't want to talk about the deal, especially not to a reporter. "The mayor is evaluating several locations. The vacant shop is just one possibility. It's not a done deal."

"After finding the Monkey King statuette, I'm sure you got this one in the bag. After all, you didn't have to turn over the artifact to the town. You could have sold it for a pretty penny in the black market."

Lucy gave him a sideways glance. What did he know about the black market for stolen artifacts? Was he pretending to know more than he did to impress her? "Sometimes, I don't know if you're here as my friend or a reporter. I don't like walking on egg-shells around you."

Damien frowned. "Yes, this could be problematic for our relationship. How about this—if I'm here professionally, I will ask you to say something for the record. Other than that, you can always trust me with your secrets." He gave her a half-smile, curving one corner of his lips. "Especially the deep dark kind."

Lucy forced herself to roll her eyes even though her heart fluttered like a hungry hummingbird. The man was just too smooth for her to handle. After spending more than half of her life in San Francisco, she should be used to men like Damien. In her former profession as an Internet marketing consultant, she had often encountered confident and powerful men who played with venture capitalists' money and women like they grew on trees. Maybe getting fired from her job a few weeks ago was a blessing in disguise.

"How's your sister?" Damien asked, taking a sip from his mug.

After an incident with her boyfriend, her half-sister needed a break from their small town. And since Lucy had an empty apartment in San Francisco, it made sense for her sister to stay there temporarily while she figured out what to do next.

And from her sister's postings on social media, it seemed the change was good for her.

"I'm surprised you have to ask," Lucy said. "The whole world knows how my sister is doing from what she posts on the Internet. The girl does not understand privacy or boundaries."

"Just trying to let you know I'm interested in your life," Damien said.

Lucy gave an unladylike snort. "I think you're interested in the train wreck that's my sister's life, just like the rest of the world."

Her sister had this misguided idea that she could become the next Internet sensation. While it was still cute at her age, in a few years, it might come back to bite her in the rear. As the older sister, Lucy should probably say something to her baby sister, but their past estrangement made it difficult for Lucy to open her mouth. She didn't want to upset their fragile relationship.

The locksmith set down his drill and twisted the handle. The door swung open. A putrid smell drifted out.

"Whoa," Damien said, frowning. "Now that's ripe."

The locksmith waved a hand over his nose, and his mouth twisted into a grimace. "You will need more than an ocean breeze to air this place out."

Lucy took an involuntary step back. In the back

of her mind, an alarm bell started ringing. She had smelled this fetid aroma before when she had discovered a dead body in her sister's apartment a few weeks ago. Please, *no more bodies*, she prayed silently to her ancestors.

The locksmith popped out the existing lock and slid in a replacement. He threw his tools into his bag and handed Lucy two duplicate keys. "Here are the keys for the new lock. I'll send you the bill in the mail, Lucy. Good luck with cleaning this place out."

Lucy shoved the keyring into her jacket pocket. The locksmith got into his car and hightailed it out of the strip mall.

Just as the locksmith's car pulled away from the parking lot, Stella pulled in. She got out of her car and came over to join Lucy in front of the vacant shop.

"Hey, you got the door open." Stella wrinkled her nose. "What's that smell?"

Damien looked at Lucy as if expecting her to charge into the vacant shop like an angry bull.

"It's coming from the shop," Lucy said, ignoring Damien's look.

"Someone should go inside to check on things and open the windows. The mayor will be here any minute," Stella said.

"Oooh, no," Lucy said, taking another step back. "I'm no superhero, nor do I claim to play one."

Stella fixed her gaze on Damien. "You're a man. Go on in there. I'm sure you want to impress Lucy."

Damien swallowed, his Adam's apple bobbing up and down. His expression was grim. "Fine. I'll take one for the team." He fixed his gaze on Lucy. "You owe me. If I go down, I want you to give me CPR." He charged into the shop.

From where Lucy stood, she couldn't see Damien. The previous tenant had pulled down the shades for the floor-to-ceiling windows. She tilted her head, straining her ears. Something scraped against metal, producing a high-pitched squeal.

"What is that?" Stella asked, covering her ears with her hands.

Lucy's heart sped up. Was someone in the shop with Damien? Maybe this person was overpowering the reporter at this moment. As she marched toward the shop, Stella cried out a warning.

Lucy glanced over her shoulder. "What—"

She collided with someone coming out of the shop and bounced off his chest. This person reached out to steady her.

Lucy straightened and glanced up at the unkempt beard and wild hair. The man towered above her, and his scent washed over her. He hadn't seen a shower in weeks. She took an involuntary step back and struggled to keep the bile from rising. She resisted the urge to brush her arms to get rid of his germs. Slung over one shoulder was a bulging knapsack. Lucy squinted at the dirty brown bag. It writhed like something was moving inside.

"Who...who are you? And what happened to Damien?" Lucy asked. Her voice came out at a pitch higher than normal.

The man staggered back like he was drunk, tripped on the curb, and fell down on the parking lot. "Help," he slurred. He clenched his hands over his heart and went still.

Lucy's jaw dropped. What—

Stella rushed to the man's side. "Hey, are you okay, buddy?"

Her cousin's action jerked Lucy out of her stupor. She crouched down on the other side of the man, keeping a wary eye on the undulating bag. "Do I need to call nine-one-one?"

Stella checked for a pulse. As the seconds crawled by, she turned ashen. She opened her mouth, but only a croak came out. She cleared her throat. "Yes. He's dead."

2

DRUNKEN SAILOR

Lucy blinked, but the image in front of her didn't go away. The strange man still lay on the asphalt of the parking lot. Did her cousin say he was dead?

The world became a fuzzy gray, and her vision narrowed until she only saw the man lying on the ground. She shook her head, hoping to clear away her confusion. The bile rose from the back of her throat again, and she swallowed the bitter tang. No, no...not again. The clanging in her head grew louder, drowning out everything.

"Lucy!" Stella called out, but it sounded as if her cousin's voice came through a bad phone connection. "Put your head between your knees and breathe."

Lucy did as instructed, feeling thick and clumsy

in her crouched position. After a few moments, her vision cleared, and she could see the tiny pebbles on the asphalt. Somehow the burlap bag had wiggled across the short distance between the dead man and Lucy. It writhed and moved against her leg. Maybe a small pet was trapped inside the bag.

As Stella returned her attention to the man, Lucy reached for the bag. The knapsack had a small pocket in the front and two buckles that held a flap over the main compartment. Lucy opened one buckle and jerked back with a yelp.

A chicken head popped out and started squawking. The beady reddish-brown eyes glared at Lucy. The bright red wattles under its beak swung from side to side.

"Is that a rooster?" Stella asked, glancing up from the man on the ground.

Lucy couldn't tell the difference between a hen and a rooster by looking at its head. "I don't know if it's a rooster, but it sure sounds like one."

"Don't let it get away. It might give us a clue to the man's identity."

Lucy eyed the chicken nervously. She didn't want to get anywhere near its beak. "The other buckle is still on. It can't get out of the bag." She glanced at the door of the vacant shop. "I better look for Damien…"

As if speaking his name invoked his presence, the reporter appeared in the doorframe. Lucy frowned. Why did it take Damien this long to come outside? Did he find something in the shop?

A vehicle pulled up next to the curb, and a door opened and slammed shut from behind them.

Lucy dragged her eyes from the door frame to the curb behind her. The mayor stared at them with his jaw wide open. She blinked. This couldn't be happening. How could she explain this to the mayor?

"What's going on over there? Did someone get hurt?" the mayor called out.

"Stella! Call nine-one-one while I stall the mayor," Lucy whispered.

Her cousin's gaze swiveled between Damien, the dead man, and the mayor. Her eyes widened at the strange situation, and a look of panic flashed across her face.

Now it was Lucy's turn to be the strong one. "Take a deep breath. It will be okay. Just call nine-one-one. Damien can take care of himself, and I will explain things to the mayor. Just talk to the dispatcher."

Stella swallowed and nodded. "Okay. I can do this."

"Why don't you make the call inside the PI office?" Lucy suggested.

Stella nodded again and got up. Lucy trotted toward the mayor.

Alexander Frasier, also known as Sander to his friends, had held the mayor position for more than a decade. He was in his late fifties with salt and pepper hair, but his full beard was snow white. With his icy blue eyes and a full belly, he was the town's year-round Santa Claus.

The butterflies in Lucy's stomach fluttered nervously. What if the mayor drove off after he found out there was a dead man in the parking lot? While most people might stare at an accident, no one wanted to be on the side of the road talking to the police.

Lucy cleared her throat. "Um, Mr. Mayor, we have a situation here. The Chicken Man came out of the vacant—"

"Who is the Chicken Man?" the mayor interrupted.

Lucy blinked. She hadn't realized she had named the dead man. "The man on the ground. He had an accident. Can we reschedule for another day? The police will probably want to talk to me and Stella. I'm sure you're too busy to wait."

"Is there anything I can do to help?" the mayor asked, his face full of concern.

Lucy shook her head. "Everything is under control here. Once we are done, I'll call your secretary to reschedule."

In the distance, sirens blared and got louder by the second.

"You might want to get out of here before the emergency vehicles block traffic," Lucy said, hoping she sounded helpful rather than desperate. The longer it took the mayor to find out about the dead man, the better. If she had more time, she might be able to neutralize the bad news.

The mayor gave the parking lot another glance. "Good point, Lucy. I don't even know CPR. Let's see if we can meet later this week. I need to decide on the museum's temporary location before the next town council meeting."

As the mayor drove off, Lucy breathed a sigh of relief. Okay, she only had to get the Chicken Man off the premises, and everything would be back to normal. She could still salvage this situation and get the lease for the town's temporary museum.

She turned back to the parking lot and saw Damien crouching over the Chicken Man. From this angle on the curb, she couldn't tell what the reporter was doing. Was he performing CPR on the Chicken Man?

Lucy marched back to the parking lot, scanning the window of the PI office. Stella was nowhere to be seen. Did she go inside the vacant shop next door? Lucy's gaze returned to Damien's back.

He reached for the knapsack, opening the

remaining buckle. The chicken's head popped out of the bag and pecked his hand. He jerked back and fell onto his rear. The chicken squawked and jumped out of the bag.

"Don't let the chicken run away. It could be evidence," Lucy called out, sprinting the last few feet. As soon as the words left her mouth, she realized her subconscious had decided this was a crime scene. After all, the Chicken Man had slurred his words and dropped dead in the parking lot. Either he was drunk or he was poisoned.

Damien glanced over his shoulder. "What?"

The chicken flapped and raced around the building, disappearing from view. Lucy ground her teeth and picked up her pace. She was not built for moving at this speed. Her breaths came out in puffs, and her lungs burned for air.

The chicken raced through the narrow strip of pavement on the side of the building that led to the back of the strip mall and the employee parking spots.

Lucy pumped her arms harder, hoping it would help propel her forward. Sweat streamed down her face. If she didn't stop soon, the emergency responders would find her collapsed on the pavement too.

The chicken squawked again and dashed for the woods behind the building. It ran, hopped, and flapped, wobbling on its skinny legs like a drunken sailor on a wooden peg.

"Hey, come back," Lucy gasped, holding onto the side of the building.

The chicken ran into the woods without a backward glance.

Lucy shook her hand in the air. Stupid chicken. She took another deep breath and straightened. Now that she was no longer focused on chasing the chicken, she realized sirens were coming from the parking lot. It was time to talk to the police.

She spun on her heels and headed back to the front of the building. A police cruiser, an ambulance, and a fire truck blocked the driveway to the shopping plaza. Between the flashing lights and the group of ladies gathered around the window at the yarn shop, it looked like they were having a block party.

The police chief, the firefighters, and Stella were huddled in a group in front of the fire truck. Two emergency medical technicians checked on the Chicken Man.

Surprisingly, Damien was nowhere in sight. Maybe the sight of a dead body up close was too much for him. Even as soon as the thought floated to the surface, Lucy dismissed it. Damien was a reporter after all. And reporters were known to see all walks of life.

Stella glanced up from the group and gestured for Lucy to join them. As Lucy crossed the parking lot, the medical technicians loaded the Chicken Man onto a gurney.

Lucy paused mid-step. Why were the medical technicians moving the Chicken Man? Shouldn't the coroner check out the body first? "Where are you taking him?" she called out.

"To the emergency room," the emergency medical technician said. He returned to his task, turning his back to her.

Lucy gaped at the EMTs. The Chicken Man was still alive? Holy Toledo! Didn't Stella have enough medical training to tell if someone was dead or alive? Weren't pharmacists as good as a doctor in some parts of the world?

The firefighters got back into their truck, waved to the crowd, and left. Max DeWitt, the police chief, trotted toward the ambulance and chatted with the EMTs.

Stella joined Lucy and whispered, "I thought only someone from the coroner could touch the body."

Lucy gave her cousin a sideways glance. "He's going to the hospital. Apparently, the Chicken Man isn't dead."

Stella flushed, a deep crimson that covered both

cheeks and her nose. "You couldn't give him a more original name?" Her voice sounded petulant.

Lucy struggled to keep the grin off her face. Her cousin was embarrassed at her misdiagnosis. "I went for the obvious. Maybe I can visit him tomorrow when I stop by to see Mom."

"I couldn't find a pulse or a heartbeat. I couldn't tell if he was drooling or if he had ingested poison. No way was I putting my lips over his," Stella said, crossing her arms defensively.

"Maybe Damien resuscitated him," Lucy said. She couldn't hide the doubt in her voice. Where was the reporter? This was big news for their small town.

"Did you see Damien give the Chicken Man CPR? He had to be pretty brave to get over the—" Stella's hand circled the air above her mouth, indicating the lower half of the man's face.

Lucy frowned. Did she see Damien give the Chicken Man CPR? After all, Damien was hunched over the Chicken Man. "I assumed he did. But if he was so concerned about saving the Chicken Man's life, why did Damien waste time by letting the chicken out?"

Stella gave Lucy a sharp look. "I know that tone. You have suspected Damien in the past of nefarious deeds, but he has turned out to be innocent. Are you reading more into things because you're looking for an excuse to keep him at arm's length?"

Heat rose to Lucy's face, and she averted her gaze. Was she afraid to have a closer relationship with Damien? "Now you're reading too much into things. Damien and I are just friends." She nodded at the police chief. "Besides, I like keeping my options open."

Stella raised an eyebrow. "Is that right? Good girl. I wouldn't want you to tie the knot with the first man that shows interest."

"I have dated plenty of men before." Lucy knew she sounded exasperated, but this was no time to talk about her love life. It was bad enough that her foster grandma was always trying to set her up, even from afar.

"Promiscuous? Even better. It's not fair that men get to sleep—"

"Look! They are leaving," Lucy cut in.

Stella glanced up to see the ambulance driving off. The police chief went to inspect the spot the Chicken Man had lain on the parking lot floor. He returned to his police cruiser, grabbed a couple of cones and crime scene tape, and blocked off the area even though the only thing visible was the empty knapsack.

Max trotted over. He was in his mid-thirties—a few years younger than Lucy—blond, well-muscled, and close to six feet tall. His moss-green eyes squinted against the sunlight, crinkling the skin around his eyes. In his uniform, he was the boy next door. Too bad he was too young for her.

"Will you still be around in a bit?" Max asked. "I want to take photos of the parking lot before folks move their cars. There's not much to see, but I want to note the man's location just the same."

Lucy nodded. "Can I go inside the vacant shop? Or do you want to see it first?"

"Let's go inside together. It's your shop, but I want to check for signs of a break-in."

"Come and get me when you're ready. Stella and I will be in the PI office," Lucy said.

They left Max to do his work. As they approached the PI office, Lucy glanced next door at the newspaper office. Through the window, she couldn't see anyone, though Damien's car was still in the parking lot. It wasn't like the reporter to be missing in action, especially in the middle of a story. Where did he go? And why didn't he want his presence known?

3

PICKING SIDES

Lucy went to the inner office and powered on her laptop, plugging in the monitor on the desk and the USB dongle for the mouse and keyboard. Since Stella had spread the word about Lucy's former profession, Lucy had gotten more work helping the local businesses revamp their websites and setting up online shopping carts than she did as a private investigator.

She logged into the hosting company and pulled up the draft of the website for the Business Chamber of Commerce. She opened the folder on her hard drive, uploading photos to the media database.

"Ah-hem," Stella said loudly from the doorway.

Lucy glanced up from the monitor. "Is Max ready for my statement?"

Stella usually occupied the desk in the front

room, acting as the receptionist when necessary, but mostly clicking on dog photos on social media. She was a dog person, which was how Lucy ended up cat sitting Raspberry for her sister. When they had an appointment, they would switch desks for the meeting with the client since Lucy was technically still a private investigator trainee.

"Do we need to talk and get our story straight?" Stella asked.

Lucy blinked. "Why would we need to collaborate on our story?"

"For one thing, we don't want to incriminate ourselves."

Lucy still didn't understand what Stella was talking about. The truth was already strange enough without having to make something up. "We didn't do anything to the Chicken Man. He'll be lucky we don't charge him for trespassing."

"He could sue us for falling on the parking lot."

"Let's worry about it when we cross that bridge," Lucy said. She didn't want to borrow trouble before she needed to. She returned to her typing, hoping her cousin would take the hint.

Stella flopped down on the client's chair across from the desk. "Do I tell the police what your boyfriend did to the Chicken Man? When I spoke to the dispatcher, I saw the whole thing through the window from inside the office."

Lucy sighed inwardly, clicked the save button, and logged out. "He's not my boyfriend. We've only gone out to dinner a few times—as friends. What was Damien doing? Searching the body?" As soon as the flippant remark came out of her mouth, she snapped it shut. Holy Toledo! Was that what he was doing?

Stella's eyes widened. "Did you see him do it too? I don't know what to tell Max. The whole thing might be innocent. I don't want to get Damien into trouble. He's such a nice man."

Lucy chewed her lower lip. If Damien had searched the Chicken Man's body and didn't find anything, it would explain why he had reached for the knapsack and, probably inadvertently, let the chicken out. But how did they know he was searching for something?

"We don't know what Damien was doing," Lucy said slowly. "We could be misinterpreting the entire thing. I don't want to accuse him without more evidence. Maybe he was looking for a wallet to get the Chicken Man's identity."

Stella nodded in agreement. "We can decide what to do after you talk to Damien. If we need to, we can tell Max we recalled this detail later."

"Why do I have to talk to Damien? Why don't you go next door and look for him?" Lucy said, recoiling inwardly.

While she thought Damien was a great guy, there was something about him that wasn't available. Like he carried a deep secret or painful past. Her past wasn't exactly perfect either, but she had been open about it, answering his questions. He, on the other hand, tended to skirt around the issue, leaving her with no more knowledge than before. Was this why she wasn't interested in a romantic liaison with the man?

Stella straightened in her chair. "But he's not my boy—"

"Lucy! Are you in here?" Max called out from the front room.

Stella got up from the client chair in front of the desk. "We're here," she called out. She lowered her voice to a whisper and said, "I'll follow your lead."

Lucy sat back in her chair. Fabulous. In other words, Stella wanted Lucy to handle the omission.

Max came into the room, his gaze shifting between Stella and Lucy. "Can I get your statements individually before we go next door to check out the vacant shop?"

Stella headed toward the doorway. "You can interview me out here. I have an errand to run after this, but Lucy can go with you."

The two of them left Lucy to stew while they spoke in the front room. With the door closed, she couldn't make out what they said. She had a feeling

Stella wouldn't mention Damien's role in the incident, leaving it up to Lucy to decide if she wanted to involve him.

A few minutes later, there was a knock on the door, and it opened. Max grinned at her. "Ready to go next door?"

Lucy got up in a jerky motion. She still hadn't decided on what to say to the police chief yet, but moving sounded like a good idea. "I thought you wanted to interview me."

"We can talk while we're looking around. Stella gave me her side of the story, and I don't think yours will deviate much from hers," Max said.

As a former assistant district attorney, Max had a good memory for details. Though he sounded casual about the interview, Lucy had to consider her words carefully if she didn't want to incriminate Damien. Darn the man for putting her in this position.

As they headed toward the vacant shop, Max asked, "Do you have any idea how the man got inside your property?"

Lucy shrugged. "The last time I checked, both the front and back doors were locked. Stella couldn't find the key, and the windows were painted shut. The locksmith just gave me the new keys."

"I'm surprised the transient picked the vacant shop. There are always people coming and going in this shopping plaza. With the mild temperature, he would be better off sleeping outside somewhere."

Lucy didn't want to tell Max the PI office wasn't generating any foot traffic. "Do you think he targeted this place in particular?"

"I guess we'll find out when he wakes up. After this, I'll swing by the hospital to see how he's doing."

She had never thought about the duties of a small-town cop. With only two full-time staff, Max probably worked a lot more hours than what the town officially paid him.

Lucy was about a foot away from the entrance when the smell hit her again. Yuck! She breathed through her mouth and followed Max inside. She glanced around, but other than a thin layer of dust on the countertop, there was nothing in the room.

The carpeted floor showed a set of footprints. From the way the footprints seemed to sway and drag on the dust, the Chicken Man was already in some distress when he staggered toward the front door, probably hoping to get help.

Lucy and Max went into the back room, which could serve as an office space or storage area for the tenant. In one corner was a restroom with a toilet and a pedestal sink, both of which were clogged. Lucy shifted her gaze from the lumps in the putrid liquid. The smell probably came from there.

In the corner opposite to the restroom was a

well-used sleeping bag and a half-eaten sandwich on plain white waxed paper and a fountain drink cup. The Chicken Man was in the middle of eating lunch. Too bad there were no business logos on the waxed paper or the cup.

Lucy breathed through her mouth. Didn't the smell bother the Chicken Man?

Max glanced around, frowning. He pulled on a pair of plastic gloves and tried the small window. It didn't budge. Next, he tried the back door. It was locked.

"Now how did he get in here?" Max mumbled to himself.

Lucy shrugged. Maybe the Chicken Man came in through the tunnel system underneath the building that connected to much of the town. But she wasn't giving away a secret the founding families didn't want the public to know.

Besides, there were no loose floorboards or holes on the ground. The only unit in the building with access to the tunnel system was the PI office. And she certainly didn't want the police going through the rest of the premises.

"On the news, they once mentioned a man climbing into a vacant building through a grease trap," Lucy said, trying to be helpful.

"There's no kitchen here, so it wasn't a former

restaurant. I don't think you'll find a grease trap outside the building."

"Let's look out in the back. Maybe we're missing something," Lucy said, gesturing to the back door.

Max opened the door and held it open for her.

As Lucy stepped through, she glanced around, looking for any clue as to how the Chicken Man got into the building. She took a deep breath of the fresh clean air.

There was a parking spot for each of the units. In the far corner of the premises was a dumpster. Since only the tenants came out here, no one made any attempt to hide the dumpster behind a concrete wall or to fancy up the place. It was just a black top lot with a few stripes designating the parking spots, and a single bulb above each door on the wall of the building.

At the edge of the pavement, thick trees and underbrush rose in front of them. As a child, Lucy had spent many happy hours playing in the woods while her grandfather and mother worked at the PI office.

Max stepped out after her. "Look at those trees. A person could easily get lost in there."

Lucy gave the sheriff a sideways glance. "Sometimes I forget that you're a city boy."

"You're a city girl, too. What's your point?"

"Touché," Lucy said with a smile.

"Sorry. I'm just a bit on edge. We have a break-in and no idea how the suspect got inside the building. And to top it off, he passed out in the parking lot. This is just strange."

"Strange things happen in the boonies," Lucy said. "And don't forget, this town has a history of pirates and smugglers, many of whom became the founding fathers." She didn't add that her family was one of them long before they crossed over to the other side of the law.

"And I'm too much of a city slicker to understand what's going on here?" Max's tone was half teasing, but his question was not.

Lucy shrugged. "I lived in the city for more than half of my life. I'm sure there are things here that I'm just not catching."

She should tell the police chief about Damien searching the body, but the words just wouldn't come out. She wanted to give the reporter a chance to explain his side of the story. After all, what kind of person would she be if she didn't help a friend out?

"Is there something else? There's this frown on your face like you're trying to puzzle out something," Max said.

"I was thinking about cleaning up the shop. When do you think I can call in a cleaning company?" Lucy said. She winced inwardly at the white lie. Max was her friend too, and she was hiding something that could potentially help him solve the break-in.

"Can you give me until tomorrow afternoon? I'll take some fingerprints and photographs. If I don't finish, I would like to come back tomorrow morning," Max said.

Lucy nodded. "That sounds fine." She left Max to do his work.

She strolled through the alley to the front of the building. When she got to the PI office, she glanced over at the newspaper office again. And like before, Damien was nowhere in sight, and there was a "Closed" sign on the door. His car was gone from the parking lot.

Stella glanced up when Lucy walked inside the office. "Did you guys find anything?"

Lucy shook her head. "There's no sign of a break-in."

"You don't think it's the tunnel sys—"

"Shhh! I don't want to reveal the secret unless we have to."

"If the Chicken Man has died, it would be good publicity for us to investigate his death."

Lucy raised an eyebrow. "To advertise Faye Investigations?"

"We need to let the town know we've still got it even with Dahlia in the hospital."

"I'm sure the Chicken Man prefers to live even if it's an inconvenience to us."

"Aren't you curious about the possible link between the Chicken Man and Damien?"

Lucy was more than curious, but she didn't want to admit it. "Not one bit."

She would try to talk to Damien tomorrow, but if she didn't hear from him by the end of the day, she would have to tell Max. Friendship or no friendship, it was the right thing to do.

4

NOT DEAD ENOUGH

The next morning, Lucy got up earlier than usual to exercise by popping in an exercise video from her mom's massive collection. Most of them were still on VHS tapes, and she had to wait while the tape rewound.

After her last two encounters with guys on the wrong side of the law, Lucy decided that even if she couldn't outrun them, she could at least put up a good fight. And Jane Fonda seemed to have such fun with her bright smile and colorful outfits on the blurry videos.

In San Francisco, walking to and from public transportation had kept her weight steady. But stress eating in the last few weeks had finally caught up to her. The reunion with her fat clothes was filled with frustration rather than joy.

When Lucy was done with the exercise video, she showered and went to the kitchen for breakfast. Raspberry, her sister's giant white and gray Maine Coon, waited by the food bowl. The cat didn't bother to greet Lucy. He just stood by his food bowl with an imperial tilt to his chin, as if waiting for the peasant to serve him.

Lucy narrowed her eyes at the cat. "Hey, Little Emperor. It wouldn't kill you to give me a fake meow in appreciation for feeding you every day, or that I have to take allergy medicine to keep you in the house."

Raspberry licked his paw as if Lucy wasn't even worth his attention.

Lucy sighed and threw her hands up in the air. It had been like this for weeks. Since her sister moved into Lucy's apartment, Lucy had become the cat's unofficial keeper. Instead of being grateful, the beast had acted as if Lucy should be the one to do all the fawning.

She shook out some Purina One into the bowl and refilled the water dish. Raspberry flicked a glance at the food and returned to his grooming. He liked the Fancy Feast, but she didn't like to feed him wet food until dinner. He was spoiled enough already.

Lucy turned on the electric kettle for hot water to make instant coffee. Her mom had a family-size bag of Nescafe in the pantry and no coffee maker. She filled a mug with two packets and made a peanut butter and jelly sandwich, using a napkin for a plate.

As Lucy ate, her thoughts wandered over to the incident yesterday. Stella was right. If they had a mystery to solve, it could be a springboard to launch Stella's credibility as the new head of the private investigation firm. Maybe they could try to figure out why the Chicken Man broke into the vacant shop. And with Lucy's natural curiosity and need for closure, she was already invested in the case.

Her estrangement with her mother had led to years of therapy. As her therapist would say, Lucy's tendency to want closure stemmed from her mommy issues. Lucy groaned in disgust because it seemed like all her thoughts naturally led back to her mother these days. She glanced at the cuckoo clock on the wall. Visiting hours at the hospital were about to start. Maybe she could check on the Chicken Man after her daily chat with Mom.

Lucy got up and rinsed her coffee cup. "Hey, Little Emperor, I'm outta here. I will see you later this evening." She checked to make sure the pet door was open, so Raspberry could go roaming if he felt like it. She had a feeling he supplemented his diet with what he found on the beach.

As she turned the corner to leave the subdivision, she noticed the light was on at Stella's house. It was only eight in the morning, and Stella was a night owl. And if someone were staying with her cousin, wouldn't Stella have mentioned this? Maybe her cousin was changing her habits too.

Lucy got on the freeway for the five-minute drive to the hospital. The two-story building was built in the late fifties. Even though it had been remodeled in the last decade, it wasn't a modern hospital with state-of-the-art doctors or equipment. She had asked about transferring Mom to a hospital in a bigger town, but the doctor didn't recommend moving the patient.

At the nurses' station, Lucy waved to Nurse Bobbi. "Any changes?"

Lucy and the nurse were about the same age, though at different stages in their lives. Nurse Bobbi was divorced with a young child while Lucy never even had a serious relationship.

From all outward appearances, they were as different as wontons and egg rolls. And yet, they became friends without effort. Nurse Bobbi's long-sleeved shirt under the scrubs didn't quite cover the tattoos on her forearms. Her blonde hair was in a no-nonsense ponytail, but her blue eyes were soft with kindness.

"I would have called you immediately if there were any changes," Nurse Bobbi said.

Lucy suppressed a sigh. Every day the answer

was the same, and yet she expected a different answer each time she walked through the door. "What about the unconscious man that was brought in yesterday? I nicknamed him the Chicken Man. Is he awake yet? He broke into our vacant shop next door to the PI office."

"You know I can't talk about other patients with you."

"I know. But if he's awake, he might talk to me, especially if it means I won't charge him for trespassing on our property."

Nurse Bobbi gave Lucy a sharp look. "You are more like your mother than you appear."

Lucy blinked in surprise. "You knew my mother before the shooting?"

"She helped track down my ex for child support. Like I said, your mother doesn't let other people push her around, and you're a lot like her." Nurse Bobbi gave Lucy a crooked smile. "I'll ask the Chicken Man if he wants to see you. He's still in and out of consciousness and weak as a new-born babe."

"He hasn't given you his name?"

"Said he forgot it. On his chart, he's a John Doe for now."

Nurse Bobbi turned and marched down the hall that led to the patient rooms. Lucy glanced around at the paperwork at the nurses' station. The hospital hadn't quite given up on paper charts yet. To Lucy, this didn't inspire trust. It was far easier to make a mistake when the nurses had to read the doctors' scribble.

A woman screamed.

Lucy whipped her gaze from the countertop and scanned the hall. Even from a distance, she shivered at the sheer terror in the scream. Her feet felt rooted to the spot, even as her mind told her to move toward the sound and offer help.

Nurse Bobbi backed out of a room, her hand covering her mouth, barely suppressing her whimpers. Her eyes were wide with terror. When her back hit the wall, she slid down onto the floor.

Seeing the normally competent nurse reduced to this state snapped Lucy out of her shock. She sprinted down the hall. When she got to the nurse, she crouched down. "What is it? How can I help?"

Nurse Bobbi jerked her head toward the voice, but it took a second for her to recognize Lucy. She pointed a trembling hand at the room. "Call the police. The Chicken Man is dead."

Lucy stiffened as if waiting for a knife to go between her shoulder blades. She turned her head slowly like a ventriloquist doll and peered into the open doorway. She swallowed the bile rising in the back of her throat. A white sheet was twisted into a rope that ended in a noose around the Chicken Man's neck as he lay in the bed.

With shaking hands, Lucy dialed nine-one-one on her cell phone, turning her back away from the crime scene. The next few hours were a blur. Someone ushered Lucy and Nurse Bobbi into the break room. Wrapped in a warm blanket and leaning back against the lumpy and worn sofa, Lucy drifted in and out of consciousness while they waited for the authorities.

She couldn't get the bloated face of the Chicken Man out of her mind. And for once, sleeping it off failed her. Each time she drifted out, she dreamed of Damien with the Chicken Man, sometimes helping him and sometimes strangling him. Each time, she woke with a jolt, only to find Nurse Bobbi cradling her head at the break table.

They had the break room to themselves, but neither one reached out to comfort the other. The overly bright fluorescent light seemed to mock them. The foldable metal chairs were hard, and the plastic tables were cheap. The air grew thicker as if feeding off their combined misery.

Lucy was too wrapped up in her fears to help the nurse. Was the Chicken Man's death her fault? If she had spoken up about Damien searching the Chicken Man yesterday, would he be alive now?

Officer Roy Martinez came into the break room. He was in his mid-twenties with brown hair and pale blue eyes. He was Hispanic but didn't speak a lick of

Spanish. Their family had lost the language two generations ago. He was also close to seven feet tall, taking up all the space and squeezing the misery from the air. He nodded at Lucy. "You holding up okay over there, Lulu?"

Lucy nodded and gave him a tight smile.

Officer Martinez shifted his attention to Nurse Bobbi. He sat down next to her and pulled out his notebook. Over the next thirty minutes, he wrangled every detail out of Nurse Bobbi in a hushed voice. Between his low baritone and the nurse's whispered replies, Lucy couldn't make out what they were saying.

She wanted to listen in on the interview, but her mind just whirled with confused thoughts, trying to figure out what she would say when it was her turn. What if Stella misinterpreted the incident yesterday? What if Damien wasn't searching the Chicken Man? If she put the reporter on the police's suspect list, what would this do to their friendship?

Nurse Bobbi pushed back from her seat and got up. Officer Martinez waited until the nurse closed the door behind her before getting up to sit next to Lucy on the sofa.

"Do you want to tell me what happened?" Officer Martinez asked.

Lucy froze. She probably had a deer in headlights look. What should she say? Should she gloss over Damien's role yesterday again?

"I would like to give my statement to Max," she said, hoping the delay would give her more time to mull over her dilemma.

"You will have to wait awhile then. Max is securing the scene," Officer Martinez said.

Lucy groaned inwardly. This was murder. She couldn't hide facts that could help the police investigation. With a sinking heart, she told Officer Martinez about Damien searching the Chicken Man.

5

ARCHIE

Later that evening, Lucy and Stella were gathered at Mom's three-bedroom Cape Cod house for a late dinner. Lucy wasn't much of a cook, unlike her cousin Raina Sun, so she made do with takeout and dinners at her foster family when she was in San Francisco. Here in the sleepy coastal town of Morro Cliff, she went back to her college diet of pasta and sandwiches. She filled Stella in on what happened at the hospital.

"Wow, I can't believe I missed all the excitement," Stella said, dipping a slice of the garlic cheese bread into the marinara sauce on her plate.

"Nurse Bobbi said the Chicken Man didn't give a name. Did he look familiar to you?" Lucy asked.

As the only pharmacist in town for the last twenty-five years, Stella knew almost everyone and

51

their ailments. In some ways, she had more private information on folks than the federal government.

Stella shook her head. "I didn't recognize him at all. It's too bad he didn't have a disease or something that required medication."

"I'll talk to Tammy tomorrow," Lucy said. The yarn shop owner was friendly with most of the younger families in town because of her children's activities and church.

"I can also ask the president of the Historical Society," Stella said eagerly.

Lucy bit the inside of her cheek to keep from smirking. The president of the Historical Society was also known as the Silver Fox among the senior citizens, and Stella had a bit of a crush on him. "Sure, why not?"

Stella blushed at the comment. For a woman in her early fifties, her cousin was as transparent as a lovesick teenager. But then again, she had spent her youth taking care of her sick parents. And there was no harm in making up for lost time as a retiree.

"Maybe we should let go of this case," Lucy said slowly. "I need to focus my energy on getting the lease for the town museum. If this doesn't work out, I will have to look for a part-time job."

"You already have a job. You're a private investigator," Stella said.

Lucy paused, considering her words carefully.

She was a trainee under Stella's license, but her cousin had never investigated a case on her own. The license was more a rite of passage. The deal was for Stella to be the figurehead at Faye Investigations until either Mom woke up or Lucy got her license and took over the family business.

"I get more business doing marketing than investigating," Lucy said.

"Don't worry, Archie," Stella said. "It's just a matter of time for the community to trust us."

"Who is Archie?"

"Archie Goodwin, the sidekick for the great detective Nero Wolfe. Haven't you read those detective books?"

Lucy shook her head. She read romance novels, but she wasn't willing to admit it out loud. "I don't have time to read. I'm always working."

Stella set down her fork and leaned forward. "You're missing out, Archie. Now back to the topic: we need to solve the Chicken Man's murder. We could use this case in a marketing campaign to advertise the new management at Faye Investigations."

"I don't think Max would look kindly on our help. And we will probably end up doing this pro bono." Lucy didn't want to be at odds with the local police.

Stella shrugged. "What difference does it make?

Business has been slow since Dahlia went into a coma."

Lucy raised an eyebrow. Slow? More like dead. Even though Stella was a Faye, she wasn't known for being a private investigator. And while Lucy grew up in town, she had been absent far too long for the folks to trust her. They would need a miracle to continue the family business.

Lucy twirled her fork in the spaghetti. If they did nothing, nothing would change. "All right. I guess we can ask a few questions."

"So, do you want to talk to Damien, or do you want me to do it?" Stella said, picking up her fork to resume eating.

Lucy took her time chewing the bite in her mouth. She didn't want to confront Damien. Their fledgling friendship might not survive the accusation. But to ask her cousin to confront the reporter made Lucy feel like a coward.

She sighed again. Hadn't she been telling everyone she wasn't interested in a relationship? It was time to walk the walk. "I will try to catch Damien in the morning. Hopefully, I'll get to him before the police do."

～

LUCY FROWNED AT THE "CLOSED" sign hanging behind the glass door of the newspaper office. She cupped her hands around her face and peered in. Though the overhead lights were off, there was enough daylight to illuminate the interior. No one was inside the office space. And the mug warmer next to Damien's computer monitor was empty, which meant he didn't even come in this morning.

She turned and strode over to A Tangled Yarn. Holly and berries trimmed the inside of the picture window of the yarn shop. The basket on the bronze wire bicycle was overflowing with red and green yarn skeins. Next to it was a four-foot Christmas tree decorated with Victorian handmade crafts. Though Morro Cliff was a small beach town with moderate temperatures and sunshine almost year round, this didn't stop the merchants from decorating like they expected a white Christmas.

Nailed to the top half of the opened Dutch door was a bronze container filled with flyers for the upcoming knitting and crocheting classes. As Lucy stepped into the shop, an old-fashioned cowbell on the doorknob clanged, announcing her arrival. Sunlight streamed in from the overhead solar tubes. On her left was a wall of built-in shelves filled with a kaleidoscope of yarn skeins. In the middle of the shop floor were circular wire racks that held knitting tools, accessories, and patterns.

On the right was a counter with a cash register. Behind the counter was a framed photo of a smiling Vietnamese family. They touched each other with love and respect—arms around shoulders and hands on backs. Lucy could never glance at the photo without her heart pausing for a beat. A person would never lack for anything in a family like that.

Tammy Nguyen sat at the barstool next to the counter, tapping on her laptop. The Vietnamese woman was about four eleven, but her two-inch heels and teased black hair gave her another three inches.

"Hi, Lucy," Tammy said. "Wasn't the other day exciting? I was glued to the window. So were all the ladies in my class. I sold a lot of yarn too."

Lucy nodded in acknowledgment. Her friend was a talker, and you couldn't rush a talker without the person getting bent out of shape.

Tammy closed the laptop and put it in the cabinet under the counter. "I heard you found Jason Albright's body at the hospital. Do you know how he died? No one knows this information. I bet Max clamped down on this detail to keep it from circulating around town." Her eyes shone with excitement.

Lucy blinked. Surely it couldn't be this easy to find the identity of the Chicken Man? "Who's Jason

Albright? Is he the man who collapsed in our parking lot?"

"Yes, that was him. He was a maintenance worker at the state park. I'd recognize that cocky face anywhere. Last summer, when my folks came down here from San Jose, we reserved a campsite big enough for an RV or camper trailer. Imagine our surprise when we showed up with a camper trailer, and the campsite was the size"—Tammy held her thumb and index finger an inch apart up in the air— "of a postage stamp."

Lucy was still reeling from the fact that Tammy just told her the identity of the Chicken Man and even his place of employment. "Whoa! Hold up." She held up her hands in the classic timeout sign. "Have you told the police the Chicken Man's name?"

Tammy gave Lucy a questioning look. "Who is the Chicken Man?"

"I meant Jason Albright. Have you told Max about Jason?"

"You named him the Chicken Man? Why?"

"You didn't see the chicken in his knapsack?"

Tammy shook her head. "Max came in the shop to ask for our statements on what happened in the parking lot, but we didn't see anything until the emergency vehicles showed up. He didn't ask if we recognized the man, so I didn't say anything. I figured they already got Jason's identity from his wallet or something."

Lucy frowned. This was unusual. Max was quite particular when it came to the details, probably from his former job as the Assistant DA. She felt a small flutter of satisfaction. Not that the two of them were in any competition. "What's your impression of Jason Albright?"

"He was a jerk. And he was also very sloppy with his work. He was supposed to look after the campsites and the trails. On that particular weekend, the trash bins were overfilled, and the restroom ran out of toilet paper."

"Any idea why anyone would kill him?" Lucy threw out the question without any expectation.

Tammy ignored Lucy's question. "I think he got fired at the end of last summer. Then I started seeing him in a city maintenance uniform around town." She frowned and thought for a moment. "How can he get fired from one job and immediately get another? Especially when there's a long wait list. He probably blackmailed somebody to get the job."

Lucy perked up at her friend's comment. Could someone have killed Jason to shut him up? "Blackmail? Any guess as to who?"

"I don't know. You're the private investigator. Isn't it your job to find this out?"

"I'm a trainee. I can't call myself a PI."

"Close enough. You have more experience than I do. Are you planning to look into Jason's death? When a healthy person dies, there's always something suspicious about it."

Lucy hesitated. While she agreed with Stella that solving this case would establish their credibility under the new management, advertising it prematurely wasn't a good idea. "Tammy, I don't know. But please don't tell anyone that I am asking questions about it. It could potentially become dangerous if the murderer knows about this."

Tammy's eyes widened. She mimed zipping up her mouth and throwing away the key. "I won't do anything that will compromise you."

Lucy didn't think her friend would either—at least not intentionally—but Tammy was a talker, and talkers tended to let things slip out.

"How do you think Jason ended up next door?" Tammy continued.

Lucy shrugged. "There were no signs of a break-in."

"The shop has gotten more foot traffic since Jason collapsed in the parking lot," Tammy said, switching subjects again.

With the town's anemic summer tourists gone, it probably didn't take much to incite curiosity. "Now imagine if we got a murder in the parking lot," Lucy said, jokingly.

"I know. That would be what I need to turn this place around."

"Is business still bad?" Lucy asked tentatively.

Tammy lost her smile. "They say most new businesses close their doors within the first three years. I think I will beat that statistic by closing my doors within the first year."

Her friend had hinted repeatedly that she wanted Lucy to help advertise her business. Lucy had declined, knowing she would have to significantly undercharge for the service. And she'd hoped Mom would wake up, allowing Lucy to return to her former life. Of course, this was weeks ago. Maybe she needed to accept that Morro Cliff was her new reality, which meant making plans beyond the next day.

"I'll help you advertise, but you have to give me free knitting lessons," Lucy said. She winced inwardly. Did those words just come out of her mouth?

Tammy's brown eyes widened in delight. A huge smile filled her face, and she leaped up from her stool, running around the counter between them. She enveloped Lucy in a bear hug. "Oh, thank you!"

Lucy stiffened. She stared down in horror at the top of her friend's head. Why was Tammy so grateful? It wasn't like Lucy just saved her life. She patted her friend's shoulder gingerly with one hand. This was awkward. "We can work out our marketing plan later. Let's go back to our earlier discussion. Who do you think killed Jason?"

Tammy pulled back, swiping a finger under one eye.

Lucy blinked. Was that a tear? She didn't realize her friend could be this emotional about such a small thing. Maybe there was more to the story behind the yarn shop. And the lease for the town museum would help with getting foot traffic to this part of town, providing a more permanent solution to her friend's problem.

Tammy leaned back on her heels, considering Lucy's words. "I'm Catholic. I don't go around accusing people, but you might want to talk to his wife."

"Why?" Lucy said. There was something about Tammy's tone that indicated Jason's marriage might not have been a happy one.

Tammy shrugged. "With the bruises he gave her, you would think Rosalynn Albright would be more than happy to see her husband dead."

6

SUITING UP

From behind Lucy, a bell chimed. She glanced over her shoulder to find Max DeWitt standing in the doorway in his cop uniform with his hands behind his back. With the morning sun streaming in from behind him, his face was in the shadow. But there was no mistaking the command in his posture.

Lucy swallowed. Yikes! Was he looking to speak to her or Tammy? She didn't want to explain why she didn't say anything about Damien searching Jason Albright in the parking lot.

Max strode up to the counter to join them. "I'm sure you ladies probably can guess why I'm here. Lucy's Chicken Man—"

"Whoa!" Lucy made the timeout sign. "What do you mean my Chicken Man? He's your problem."

Tammy snickered. "I was just telling Lucy about Jason Albright."

Max gave Lucy a sideways glance, but he addressed Tammy. "Is that the Chicken Man's name?" When Tammy nodded, he continued, "Anything else you can tell me about him?"

Before Tammy could open her mouth, Lucy backed away from the two of them. "I better get going. The two of you probably have a lot to talk about. You wouldn't want a civilian listening in on police business."

Max turned and narrowed his eyes at her. "That didn't seem to stop you before." His tone was professional without a hint of friendliness.

Tammy's eyes widened from behind Max's back. She knew all about Lucy's friendship with the police chief.

Lucy swallowed. He was annoyed with her, all right. "Yep, none of my business."

"Don't go too far," Max said, his tone brisk. "I want to talk to you next."

A bead of sweat popped up on the small of Lucy's back. She gave him a tight-lipped smile and fled the yarn shop. As she stepped onto the sidewalk, she glanced longingly at her car. Maybe she should hop in and ride off into the sunset.

When Lucy strolled into the PI office next door, Stella was in the front room, replying to a forum bulletin board post on the computer. The town folks still liked the anonymity of using an alias rather than their real name in a forum board.

Stella glanced up and waved Lucy over. "Look at all these comments about the Chicken Man's death in the Morro Cliff group."

Lucy scanned through the comments. Half of them made no sense at all and several were rants against the homeless population. Was Jason homeless? With his wife? There were no signs of another person in the vacant shop. "Did you read anything useful?"

Stella shook her head. Her eyes were still glued to the screen. "Not yet, but I am monitoring the situation."

"Did you get a chance to talk to Dave Michaels?" Lucy asked.

Stella blushed, and she continued to focus on the monitor like it was a lifeline. "Not yet."

Lucy narrowed her eyes. Her cousin had seemed eager to approach Dave Michaels last night. It was well into the afternoon already. "Please don't tell me that you're too nervous to approach the Silver Fox?"

She intentionally used Dave Michaels's nickname to gauge Stella's reaction. The female senior citizens in town voted the Historical Society president as the most eligible widower last year.

Stella turned even redder. "Of course not. Why...why would I be afraid to approach him?"

"You tell me."

"There's nothing to tell."

"Uh-huh."

"Seriously, there's nothing."

Lucy smiled. Oh, her cousin had it bad for Dave Michaels, all right. "Okay." She filled Stella in on her conversation with Tammy.

"I know Rosalynn Albright," Stella said. "She used to pick up her mom's medication, but I think her mom passed away a couple of years ago."

"Tammy implied that Jason...um...abused her," Lucy said, uncomfortable with the topic.

Stella frowned in thought and shook her head slowly. "I don't think so."

"You didn't see her covering up bruises?"

Stella shook her head again. "I didn't know Jason, but I knew Rosalynn and her mother. From the small talk I had with Rosalynn, he seemed to adore her. They were high school sweethearts before getting married."

Lucy had assumed that Tammy was a reliable source of information, but this didn't mean it was true. At the same time, neither could she assume that Stella remembered the details of folks' small talk correctly. After all, she probably talked to several people every day for years in the pharmacy. "I think we need to talk to Rosalynn."

Stella gave Lucy a sharp look. She opened her mouth but was interrupted by the chirping of an incoming text message.

Lucy reached into her purse, pulled out the device, and tapped on the message app. "It's from Damien. He wants to talk to me alone at the lighthouse." She glanced at her cousin. "I have to go."

Stella shook her head. "Not like that, you aren't. Let's wire you up, so I can listen in from the car. His disappearance in the last two days is mighty suspicious. As much as I like the guy, if he is somehow tangled up with the Chicken Man, I don't want you alone with him."

Lucy bit her lower lip. Her cousin was right, but it didn't make the decision easy. This implied that Damien might have been lying to her all along.

She liked to think she was a better judge of character, but she wasn't infallible. But if Damien did turn out to be something other than what he seemed, it would shake her to the core. It'd been a long time since she let a man get this close to her. "Okay. Wire me up. But do it quickly. Max will be coming over to talk with me once he's done with Tammy."

They retreated into the inner office and closed the door behind them. Stella opened the closet, which served as equipment storage for them. Lucy removed her sweater and T-shirt, leaving only her bra on.

Stella glanced over at Lucy and whistled. "Serious on the outside, but freaky on the inside. I really like that hot pink bra with the black lace trim. Where did you get it?" She quickly pulled out the equipment and started taping the wire to Lucy's body.

Lucy blushed. "It's something I picked up from my foster grandma. It's a Chinese thing. There's always this external pressure to fit in and to be respectable, so you express yourself with fancy lingerie. And I didn't buy this, my foster grandma did."

Stella snickered. "I figure your grandma is a bad influence on you. When is she coming to visit again?"

Lucy laughed out loud. The last time the bosom buddies worked together, Stella got a new makeover. The next time, who knew what the two of them would come up with? "No idea."

Knock! Knock!

"Lucy!" Max called out from the other side of the door. "Are you in there?"

Lucy's eyes widened. "Just a minute. Don't come in. I'm not fully dressed."

Stella helped Lucy into her T-shirt and sweater.

She stepped back and eyed Lucy critically and nodded. "We need to get rid of him."

Lucy took a deep breath and opened the door. "That was quick. I thought Tammy would talk your ear off." Her voice came out a decibel higher than normal.

From the doorway, Max's gaze shifted from Lucy to Stella and back again. "Do I want to know what's going on here?" he asked slowly and took a step back.

Stella brushed past him and went into the outer room. "Don't be silly, Max. I was helping Lucy with a wardrobe malfunction."

Lucy, who was following behind the two of them, stumbled and fell forward. She grabbed hold of Max's back to keep from face planting onto the floor. When she straightened, she mumbled, "I'm sorry."

"Where are the two of you going?" Max asked, his gaze shifting between Lucy and Stella.

"We have an appointment with a potential client," Lucy said. She felt slightly guilty for lying, but she wasn't ready to have a tête-à-tête with the police chief about Damien and his whereabouts. Besides, if she didn't leave soon, she might never find out what Damien was up to.

Max studied her for a long moment. "And this important client can't wait?"

Lucy stiffened her back to keep from squirming

under his intense gaze. While those eyes might drag a confession from others, she wasn't a criminal. She shouldn't feel guilty.

"Of course not," Stella cut in. "You know how slow business is for us since Dahlia's hospitalization." She glanced at Lucy. "We have to go. I'll wait for you in the car outside while you lock up."

Lucy gave Max a sideways glance. "Let's have a rain check for tomorrow." She held the door open.

Max stepped out. "How about dinner later tonight?" he whispered.

Lucy hesitated. Under normal circumstances, she would be all over this, happy with a chance to pump the police chief for information. But there was nothing normal about this murder, and she still hadn't figured out if her loyalties lay with Damien—who better have a good reason for what he did—or with the law.

"I don't think we can be too chummy while you're investigating this case," Lucy said slowly. She couldn't believe these words were coming out of her mouth. "We wouldn't want folks in town to think you're showing favoritism."

Max blinked and considered her words. "Did you kill Jason Albright?"

Lucy recoiled. "I didn't kill him. I don't even know the man."

"What about your best bud?"

"Who? Why would my best friend drive from San Francisco to our small town to kill a city maintenance worker?"

"I meant Damien North. Where is he? I have been trying to talk to the guy for the last two days. His office is closed, and he's not home."

Lucy shrugged. She had to get going soon, or Damien might get spooked and disappear before she got there. "I don't know. I'm wondering the same thing." She glanced at her watch. "I have to go. I'll catch up with you later."

She got into the car and turned on the car engine. Max still stood next to the PI office, watching her. She held up her hand and wiggled her fingers in a half-hearted wave and pulled out of the parking lot. If Damien didn't have a good excuse for his sudden disappearance, she would have to turn him over to the police.

7

INDIANA JONES WANNA BE

Lucy kept glancing at the rearview mirror during the entire drive out to the light-house. Her shoulders and chest were tight from the tension. The transmitter box in the small of her back was an uncomfortable reminder that she didn't know Damien well enough to trust him completely.

The few times they had gone out to dinner or a movie weren't enough to explore each other's past, present, or future. As an Internet marketing consultant, she had relied on data and statistics to make multimillion-dollar advertising campaigns, but when it came to matters of the heart, she was no better than a teenager. She wasn't sure she could trust her gut when it came to Damien.

And unfortunately, Stella couldn't provide any

guidance either, having remained single her entire life. Lucy didn't know if there was some great romantic disappointment in her cousin's past, which made giving up her life to take care of her aging parents the easier choice.

Lucy dragged her thoughts back to the current situation. After all, romance wasn't the reason why she was willing to meet Damien. She had to know if her judgment was compromised because she had warm feelings for this man. And if he was in trouble, it was her duty as a friend to help him.

The parking lot was empty. Since it was the off-season and mid-afternoon—which meant the locals were at work or in school—they probably had the whole cliff to themselves. Stella stayed in the car, and Lucy made her way along the meandering dirt path to the lighthouse and the keeper's cottage. Even from this distance, Lucy had to squint against the bright glare of the sun's reflection on the ocean waves. The glass lens on the top of the lighthouse winked at her approach.

Lucy had no idea if Damien was staying at the lighthouse or hiding in one of the nearby sea caves. Was he running from the law? Her heart rate sped up at the thought. Could she help a criminal? She didn't know the answer to these questions.

When she got to the lighthouse, she scanned the surroundings, but there were no signs of the reporter. "Damien," she called out. "It's Lucy. I'm alone."

The dilapidated circular stone column rose in front of her. Up close, she could see moss clung to the nooks on the surface. There were notches cut into the stone like the medieval openings for arrows against an invading army. They were much too small for a grown man to squeeze through. The original copper roof was gone. Probably stolen at some point in its long history.

The wooden door of the lighthouse was locked. If Damien was hiding out somewhere, it would most likely be at the keeper cottage. She turned right and trotted the few yards to the only other structure on the cliff.

The Historical Society had removed the wood planks boarding up the house and replaced the broken glass with modern glass made to imitate period glass. They had also replaced the front door with something sturdier but used the original hardware. In order for Damien to get in, he would have to break one of the new windows. And he wasn't the kind of person who would damage other people's property. He had a healthy respect for the historical value of things.

"Damien!" She called out again. "It's Lucy. If you don't come out, I'm leaving." If this turned out to be a wild goose chase, she would definitely have some choice words for him.

"I'm in the garden behind the house," Damien whispered.

Lucy peered at the corner of the house. She took a deep breath and tiptoed around the building.

Damien was sitting on the low rock wall that protected a patch of dirt and weeds from the elements, drinking from a thermos. It had been decades since any vegetable had grown here. He crooked a finger at Lucy in the universal "come here" signal. "Anyone missed me yet?"

"The entire world is looking for you. What did you do? Why are you in hiding?" Lucy meant to use a teasing tone, but it came out more serious than she intended.

Damien blinked, considering her words. "I'm not hiding from anyone. I'm trying to avoid Jason Albright until he moves onto his next scam. I want no part in what he's proposing."

Lucy took a step closer. She wanted to ask why he had searched Jason's pockets. "Sounds like you know Jason pretty well. What does he want with you?"

Damien shrugged, but his finger tapped the bottom of his thermos. "Jason is a small-time criminal. He had a business proposition that he thought might interest me."

Lucy noticed the nervous finger tap. "And it didn't?"

Damien shook his head. "Not even for a second."

"I still don't understand why you feel like you need to hide. After all, it's not like Jason can force you into doing something you don't want to do."

"Yes and no. He convinced my crazy rich uncle to support his proposal. And since I'm my uncle's business representative locally..." Damien shrugged. "It's better to avoid the discussion entirely."

Lucy nodded. This made sense. "If you avoid Jason long enough, you're hoping he will find another business partner."

"Bingo."

"Then why did you search Jason's pockets? Stella saw the whole thing from the PI office."

"I was afraid Jason might have a business card or something that links him back to me or my uncle. There was nothing in his sleeping bag either, so we're in the clear."

Lucy studied Damien for a long moment. Everything he said sounded plausible, and much of it might even be true, but he was hiding something from her. And who used business cards these days? "Shouldn't you worry about being in his phone's contact list instead? Do shady people use business cards?"

Damien scowled at Lucy. "I'm not shady."

Lucy held up both hands, palms out. "I believe you." *Yeah, right,* she thought to herself.

"And he doesn't have my personal number. I think that's why he was hiding out in the vacant shop, hoping to catch me."

Lucy blinked. So Jason might have targeted the shop on purpose. "What kind of business are we talking about? Jason isn't exactly known to be an upstanding kind of guy."

"I'd rather not say."

"Oookay," Lucy said, dragging the word out. "Then why am I here?"

"I was hoping you could give me some information. Is Jason out of the hospital yet? Can I return to the newspaper office without worrying about this guy grabbing hold of me?"

Lucy narrowed her eyes. She couldn't keep the frown off her face. Normally Damien was the first person to know all the news and rumors flying around town. He monitored the forum postings even more religiously than Stella did. "You haven't heard the news? As the town's only reporter, I thought you would be more on the ball."

"I'm trying to keep a low profile. And I can't get a good cellular signal out here."

"Uh-huh."

Damien looked disappointed. "You don't believe me."

"Where are you staying? In a sea cave? It just seems kind of extreme when you could stay home and not open the door."

"Now that Jason has gotten an interested investor, he is like a dog going after a bone. He even squatted at the vacant shop to keep an eye on me."

"How do you know his wife didn't kick him out?" Lucy said. "He might have just needed a place to crash for the night."

"In that case, why didn't he go somewhere a little bit more comfortable? I'm sure he could crash at a friend's place. No, he's at the vacant shop because he still thinks the business proposition might make him millions."

Lucy sighed. This circular logic was getting them nowhere. "What do you want from me? If you can't tell me the truth, how do I know I can trust you?"

"And how do I know I can trust you?"

"Touché."

They were both silent for a long moment, staring into each other's eyes. Lucy had to admit that he had a point. While they had been tested in the last few weeks, they didn't have enough time together to cement their friendship. Trust didn't come easy for Lucy. It never had.

"Are you wearing a wire?" Damien finally asked.

Lucy's eyes widened, and she quickly tried to hide her surprise. Should she come clean? After all, trust was a two-way street. "How did you know?"

"Stella's idea?"

Lucy gave him a sheepish smile. She reached behind her and removed the transmitter. The wires would have to remain in place until she had the privacy to take off her shirt. She put the device into her purse. "Happy now?"

Damien shook his head and patted a spot next to him on the stone wall.

Lucy did an undignified scramble up the three-and-a-half-foot wall and flopped down with a sigh. She should spend more time with those Jane Fonda tapes.

Damien slung an arm around her shoulders. "I have a secret identity."

Lucy glanced up at him and raised an eyebrow. "So which one are you, Bruce Wayne or Clark Kent?"

"Neither. I'm more of an Indiana Jones."

"An archeologist?"

"A treasure hunter."

Lucy's mind whirled as all the pieces snapped into place. "Jason wants you to help him steal the Monkey King statuette. Are you a collector or a broker for stolen goods?" She paused, considering his uncle's role in the business proposition. "No, wait. Your rich uncle is the collector."

Damien's mouth dropped. "How did you do

that?"

Lucy chuckled and wiggled her fingers. "Magic." While her tone was light, she wondered what other illegal activities Damien might be involved in. "Is the newspaper a front for your questionable activities?"

"Whoa! Your mind is going in the wrong direction. My uncle does not buy artifacts without the right provenance."

"Then how are you a treasure hunter?"

"My uncle has funded expeditions looking for treasure, and sometimes I join them to watch out for my uncle's interest. And the newspaper job isn't a front for anything. My uncle bought the business when the previous owner retired."

Lucy studied Damien for a long moment. She didn't know much about treasure hunting and the private collections of the ultra-rich, but she didn't think it was the Wild West anymore. Folks couldn't just go into an archaeological site in a developing country and bring home what they dug up. And she didn't have time for a long debate on the legality of stolen artifacts. She gave the reporter a sideways glance. "Jason Albright died in the hospital yesterday."

Damien stiffened next to her. He blinked several times as if he was having a hard time processing her words. When he finally spoke, it came out in a croak. "How?

"Someone fashioned a noose from the sheet and hung him from the medical equipment. It was not suicide."

"Wasn't he in the hospital?"

"Yes, but the hospital doesn't have around-the-clock security. It's relatively easy to sneak past the nurses' station when they are busy making the rounds."

Damien sat perfectly still for several moments. He hopped off the wall and paced in front of Lucy. "I don't have to hide from Jason anymore." He paused, running a hand through his hair. "But I might be a murder suspect."

"Why did you say a murder suspect?" Lucy called out, hoping to get his attention.

Damien stopped pacing and spun around. "I'm assuming you told Max about me searching Jason's pockets."

Lucy squirmed in her seat. "I'm sorry, but I had to tell him the truth."

"And you did the right thing. I don't expect you to lie for me. But it sure makes me look suspicious." Damien stared intently into her eyes. "I didn't kill Jason Albright. My past is not so sordid that I had to shut him up. Do you believe me?"

Lucy studied Damien for a long moment. As crazy as it sounded, she did believe him. "Yes. And we have to solve this murder to clear your name."

8

GOOD OLD DAYS

When Lucy opened the driver's door, Stella glanced over in relief from the passenger seat.

"Here you are. You almost gave me a heart attack. Why did you turn off the transmitter?" Stella asked. Her tone was tight like she was both annoyed and anxious at the same time.

Lucy blushed. She hadn't considered how her cousin would react to the sudden radio silence. "Sorry. Damien knew you were listening, and he wasn't willing to give me honest answers until I disabled the device." She frowned at a sudden thought. "Weren't you supposed to be my backup? How come you didn't run out there with guns blazing?"

Stella rolled her eyes. "First, I don't own a gun. Second, I've known Damien long enough that I trust him."

"Then why did you want me to wear a wire in the first place? It's so uncomfortable with the transmitter on my back." She removed her shirt and peeled off the tape for the wire.

Stella gave Lucy a sheepish smile. "It was my only chance to eavesdrop on the two of you."

Lucy put her shirt back on. If Stella turned out to be one of those gossip-mongering retirees, Lucy would have to cut her off. "Why?"

Stella shifted in her seat, adjusting and readjusting the seatbelt across her shoulder. "I'm sorry, my dear. I want you to find somebody because I don't want you to end up alone like me."

Lucy studied her cousin for a long moment. How did she acquire all these matchmakers in her life? First, her foster grandma, and now, Stella. Fabulous. Luckily, they couldn't tie her up and force her down the aisle. "You're a strong independent woman— financially secure and emotionally balanced. I will be lucky if I grow up to be like you."

Stella blushed at the compliment. "Quite frankly, I don't want to be alone anymore."

"What about me? Am I not good enough company for you?" Lucy teased.

"My dear, you are not going to be here forever. Once your mother is back on her feet, you'll be back in the city."

"And then you'll have Mom to keep you company."

"Your mom and I care for each other, but we are not close. There's a big enough age gap between us that she has only seen me as the pesky younger cousin growing up. And now, as adults, she still sees me in the same light. I don't think we can get close. But with you, I feel like I found a friend."

Lucy reached across the console and patted her cousin's hand. "I'm not going anywhere anytime soon. As for my love life, fate can take care of that." She started the car engine and backed out of the parking spot.

"You're spitting distance from forty. You won't have much time left to have children. I just don't want you to regret missing this opportunity." Stella paused and thought for a moment. "Maybe you can have a baby without the husband."

Lucy snickered. Oh, how the times had changed. When her mother had Lucy decades ago as an unwed mom, the town had shunned her. "Sorry to burst your bubble, but I am not interested in children of my own." Because of her troubled childhood, she always knew she would never want children. "Breanne is our only hope for passing on the family business to the next generation."

Stella sighed as if she were resigned to the disappointing outcome. "Well, while you were having your tête-à-tête with Damien, I made some phone calls. The mayor has half an hour for you this afternoon. I have a meeting with Dave Michaels." She blushed and glanced at her watch to hide the burning cheeks.

Lucy smiled inwardly. Stella should worry about her own love life.

"We have just enough time for lunch before our appointments," Stella said.

During the drive to the Shoreline Bakery, Lucy filled Stella in on Damien's dealings with Jason Albright. "The details about Damien's rich uncle are hush-hush. I don't think he wants this information known around town."

Stella nodded. "Got it. The police will think Damien's actions are suspicious."

"Damien came to the same conclusion," Lucy said with a sigh. "We have to help him. As the prime suspect and a reporter, folks wouldn't want to talk with him. The two of us are a neutral third party."

"And Faye Investigations would get all the credit for solving this case." Stella sat back in her seat with a wide grin. "And I will be just as good of an investigator as Dahlia, even though my branch of the family isn't in the succession line."

Lucy gave Stella a sideways glance. Ah, so this was the heart of the issue between Mom and her cousin, a silent one-sided rivalry that wedged out trust and honesty.

The Faye Family Trust was set up so only the eldest son in a long line of eldest sons could inherit the family business and the wealth, much like how things were arranged in traditional Chinese culture. Except the ancestors didn't account for the last two generations—where all the Fayes were women.

IT TOOK Lucy five minutes to drive through the two stoplights to the town square. She parked at the public lot across from the police station. As they made their way across the cobblestone plaza with its Italian-inspired water fountain, Lucy wondered once again how come the hordes of Southern California residents hadn't discovered the town. Maybe it was the lack of beach access. The town only had about a two-mile beach with the rest of the coastline filled with jagged cliffs and sea caves. The weather was also unreliable with fog rolling in even in the summer months.

The current mayor had an ambitious dream of bringing more tourism to the area. However, not everyone in town supported this idea. Once the wealthier Southern California residents discovered the charm of this place, they could snap up homes in the area and drive up prices, forcing folks who had been here for generations to move out. And yet, without an infusion of money, the town didn't have the funds needed to replace much of its infrastructure or support its aging population. It was too bad the younger folks moved away to cities for college and jobs.

At the Shoreline Bakery, Lucy and Stella got behind the long line that wrapped around to the outside of the building. With only Starbucks as their competition, the bakery raked it in on the local business. After Lucy and Stella got their sandwich and coffee orders, there was still no table available for them. They crossed the street and made their way to the water fountain. The Christmas tree in the middle of the square blocked their view to the Pacific Ocean.

Halfway through lunch, Stella straightened and tapped Lucy on the shoulder. Her gaze cut to a woman walking down the steps of City Hall. "That's Rosalynn Albright."

Rosalynn was one of those women who met middle age too soon. Her lavender cable-knit sweater did little to hide her thickening waist, but her legs remained slim in her skinny jeans. The freckles and moles on her skin proved that her tan came from the sun rather than a bottle. Gray eyes, wide black brows, and a helmet of glossy black hair, which definitely came from a bottle.

"Can you introduce us?" Lucy asked. This probably wasn't a good time for the introduction, but it was too good of an opportunity to pass up. After all, the spouse often had the best motive for killing the victim.

Stella stood up and waved both arms overhead like she was trying to land an airplane. "Hey, Rosalynn. Over here."

Rosalynn Albright paused mid-step. She glanced at Stella and then shifted her gaze to Lucy. She came over and studied Lucy. "Do I know you from somewhere? You seem familiar."

Now that the other woman mentioned it, Lucy found her vaguely familiar too. They were of the same age. Did they go to school together? "When I was growing up in town, my name was Lucy Faye. Now I use my dad's last name, so I am Lucy Fong."

Rosalynn snapped her fingers together. "So you are my old friend."

Lucy gave the woman an apologetic shrug. "I'm sorry. I had a lot of issues at home in my childhood, so I don't remember much of my school life. When were we friends?"

"Well, I also look different now too. When we were friends in seventh grade, I had these Coke-bottle glasses and braces. Maybe you've forgotten about me because you had a lot more friends than I did."

A memory floated to the surface of Lucy's mind. Her nostrils flared from the memory of the sweaty gymnasium. She could almost hear the squeal of tennis shoes on the waxed floor. "We had gym class together."

Rosalynn broke into a beaming smile. "You do remember me."

Lucy was embarrassed to say that the only thing she remembered was a skinny kid with thin legs in baggy shorts and big frizzy hair. A stereotypical nerdy kid. She had no memory of them spending time together outside of class. "Yep, those were the good old days," she said with a tinge of sarcasm.

Rosalynn laughed out loud. "Boy, am I glad those good old days are long gone."

"Me too," Lucy said. Holy Toledo! She had an *in* with Rosalynn. She could question her under the guise of catching up with an old friend.

Stella's gaze shifted between the two of them. "I guess we don't need introductions around here." She gave Lucy a significant look. "I'll leave you two girls to catch up. I have to get going. I've got a date." Her eyes widened as she suddenly realized her word choice. She flushed beet red. "I meant I have an appointment." She turned abruptly and marched off.

As the two of them watched Stella scurry off, Rosalynn leaned closer to Lucy and whispered, "She dates? I thought she was a confirmed old maid."

"Old maid is such an old-fashioned term. I like to think she's single and unattached," Lucy said. "Have you heard of the Silver Fox?"

Rosalynn's eyes widened. "Are they together? Now that would break a lot of the ladies hearts around here. When my mom was alive, she had a soft spot for him too, even though she was very much in love with my dad."

"Well, I don't think they're an item, but I would like them to be."

"Matchmaking? It's so like you, Lucy, always helping a friend out."

Lucy found it strange that Rosalynn's impression of her was so favorable. Was Lucy kind as a child? All she remembered were the arguments with her stepfather that finally led to her running away and showing up at her paternal uncle's doorstep in San Francisco.

"How are you holding up, Rosalynn? I heard

about what happened to Jason," Lucy said. She softened her tone, hoping to convey sympathy.

Rosalynn glanced behind her and lowered her voice. "Jason and I have been separated for over a year. I'm upset over his death, but I'm not grieving. I don't know if you understand what I'm trying to say."

"Actually I think I do. I was upset when my stepfather died, but I didn't grieve for him either. A part of me was even glad he was gone, so I didn't have to deal with him anymore, but another part of me felt guilty for feeling that way."

Rosalynn nodded eagerly. "Yes, you described my feelings perfectly. The last few years of our marriage were difficult."

Lucy's thoughts wandered back to Tammy's comment about Jason smacking Rosalynn around. Was there any truth to this rumor after all? How could she bring this up naturally in a conversation? "What was Jason like? I heard that he...liked to talk with his fists."

"Jason never laid a hand on me, despite what people thought. I was his first girlfriend, and he adored me." Rosalynn blushed. "I was the one who outgrew him."

"Everyone said he abused you. I'm glad that is not the case. I wonder how the rumor started," Lucy said. She wondered if Tammy was the one who started the rumors.

"You know how this town talks. All it takes is for me to show up at a function with a bruise on my shin."

Lucy knew all too well how this town talked. "Did Jason go to school with us? I don't remember him at all."

"No, he was an army brat. After his parents divorced, his mother settled in town with him. He was fifteen. By that time, you had already left town."

Lucy gave Rosalynn a cheeky smile. "So you reeled in a younger man. You old cougar."

They both laughed. It was laughable now, but a year made a big difference in high school.

"What brings you to City Hall?" Lucy asked.

"Paperwork. Technically, I'm still married to Jason."

"His family is not around to handle this?"

Rosalynn shook her head. "His mother is gone now, and I don't know how to get in touch with his dad. It's the least I can do for the poor guy."

"Do you know why he was camping out at the vacant shop next to the PI office?"

Rosalynn frowned for a moment. "Oh, yeah. I'd forgotten about Faye Investigations. Is it still open for business?" she asked tentatively. "I heard about your mother. Until now, I didn't know you were back in town."

"Stella is a licensed investigator. I'm helping out at the office until my mom gets back on her feet." All of which was technically true. Lucy didn't think her role as the unlicensed investigator should be public knowledge. She needed the community to trust her first. After all, Lucy had been gone for so long that folks might consider her as an outsider.

"Jason gave me a fright when he popped out of the vacant shop," Lucy continued, hoping Rosalynn would take her bait and run with it. "How do you think he got in? The shop was locked up."

"Jason apprenticed with a locksmith for a while. I thought he would make a career out of it, but he actually wanted to pick locks. I thought I could reform the bad boy, but bailing him out of jail for petty crimes got old real fast."

Lucy grimaced. Oh, she knew all about reforming the bad boy. "Been there and got my stamp on the frequent buyer card."

The two women shared a sheepish smile.

"Why was Jason in hiding? I'm assuming that's what he was doing," Lucy said.

"You're not going to believe this," Rosalynn said. "The FBI contacted Jason because his name was found in an assassination market on the dark web. Apparently, someone paid some kind of crypto-currency to kill him." She rolled her eyes. "So he went into hiding."

Lucy's jaw dropped. Most assassination markets were scams set up to rip off the users angry at their bosses or neighbors. Once the funds were transferred over, the "assassin" would have a failed attempt and need more funds to complete the mission. Some gullible users would then give the site more crypto-currency. It was as good a scam as winning the Nigerian lottery. And unlike a credit card transaction, the user couldn't call their bank to reverse the charges since crypto-currency was designed to be untraceable.

"Why would the FBI contact Jason? Until a significant amount of money changes hands, do they have the resources to follow-up on stuff like this?"

"I don't know, but somebody transferred over five thousands dollars of this crypto-currency."

Lucy's eyes widened. So money did change hands. Now this was something else entirely. "Do you have any idea who would want to kill Jason?"

"He stole anything that wasn't nailed down, but this wasn't enough reason for someone to kill him. But he also had a tendency to know...secret things about people."

"Did he blackmail them?"

"I don't know, but he got a kick out of knowing things."

"Is there a reason why you two didn't get a divorce?"

"He wouldn't give me one. He was dragging his feet even though we both had lawyers working on it. I'd been trying to finalize the divorce for almost two years."

Lucy blinked. Was this reason enough for Rosalynn to kill her husband? "Jason was found with a chicken. Why would he have a chicken with him?"

"It was his therapy chicken. Most people have cats or dogs, but Jason went with a rooster."

"Let me get this straight. Jason went into hiding because he was afraid someone wanted to assassinate him. And he took his therapy chicken with him to help manage the stress?" It took all of Lucy's willpower to keep a straight face.

Rosalynn shrugged. "Your guess is as good as mine." She glanced at her watch. "Look at the time. I have to get back to work. My lunch break is almost over."

"Sorry for holding you up. Where do you work? We should catch up sometime."

"At the hospital. I do their insurance billing."

They pulled out their cell phones and exchanged numbers.

"I'll give you a call soon. Maybe we can get a coffee together," Lucy said.

As Lucy watched Rosalynn make her way to the

public parking lot, she couldn't help but wonder if Rosalynn killed Jason. After all, since they were technically married with no other family around, she would be his heir. And not only did she have a motive, but she had access to the victim. She could have come out of the billing office, strolled through the corridor to Jason's hospital room, and killed him during her coffee break.

9

PRO BONO

clerk led Lucy to the mayor's reception room. A woman in her late fifties leafed through a decorating magazine on the mahogany desk in front of her. On her left, a plush leather sofa squatted in front of the accent wood panel wall. Behind her, the inner office door was closed. The clerk introduced Lucy to Abigail Frasier and left.

"Frasier? Are you related to the mayor?" Lucy asked with open curiosity.

"He's my husband," Abby said, getting up from the desk to shake Lucy's hand. Her grip was solid and firm. "Please call me Abby. I'm named after my grandmother, and she's Abigail."

She was tall and willowy. Wispy mud-brown

bangs partially hid her narrow face. The thick layer of concealer underneath her brown eyes couldn't hide the supersized eye bags. In her too big butterscotch sheath dress, she looked nothing like Mrs. Claus.

"His secretary is on vacation this week, so I'm helping out," Abby continued.

"That's nice of you," Lucy said. She wondered if Abby was on the payroll, but it seemed rude to ask.

"We are waiting for one more person," Abby said.

"Stella isn't coming."

"We're waiting for Calla Louie. Not Estelle," Abby said. "Do you know her?"

Lucy shook her head. Abby sure didn't extend the same courtesy to someone else for a person who insisted on using a cute nickname. Stella had inherited her name from her great-grandma, and Lucy knew her cousin hated it.

"Calla represents the Chinese community in town," Abby said. "She is not old enough to be an elder, so I'm not quite sure what her exact role or title is."

Lucy frowned. Was Calla Louie her competition for the temporary museum lease? The name sounded vaguely familiar, like she had heard it recently. "Is she a town employee?"

Abby shook her head. "No, she works for the State Parks."

Lucy's eyes widened in recognition. She was Jason Albright's former coworker. "Why is she at this meeting? I thought we are here to discuss the lease for the temporary museum."

Abby wrung her hands. "Oh, dear. Sander probably didn't communicate his idea to Stella. Give me a second."

She turned and knocked on the closed inner office door. Without waiting for an answer, she opened it and stepped inside, closing it behind her. A few seconds later, Abby came back out. "Sander wants to talk to you, my dear, before Calla gets here." She held open the door for Lucy.

Sander glanced up from the report on his desk and gestured for Lucy to come into his office. After Lucy stepped inside, Abby closed the door after her, retreating back to the secretary desk.

The mayor's office was distinctly male—a mahogany desk, mahogany credenza, and a black leather swivel chair. Even the two padded leather chairs with metal hardware in front of the desk were masculine. The wood panel accent wall behind the desk matched the one on the outside. The potted fern and framed photographs on top of the credenza softened the appearance of the room.

While Sander set aside the report, they

exchanged pleasantries. He folded his hands over his jolly stomach and leaned back on his chair as if they were having a casual chat. "I am so glad we have a few minutes to ourselves, Lucy. I heard that Jason Albright was murdered at the hospital."

Lucy groaned inwardly. Was the mayor a gossip-monger too? "I was visiting my mom when the nurse found the body."

Sander stroked his white beard. "This town is going to pot. You come back to town, and the dead bodies start showing up." He smiled to show that he was teasing. "Maybe you should have stayed in the big city."

Lucy gave him a deadpan stare. "The same could be said about the police chief."

Sander burst out laughing, jiggling his stomach. Lucy joined him half a heartbeat later.

When they finally got control of themselves, Sander said, "Some folks wouldn't want the museum associated with murder."

Lucy's heart sank. She needed the lease to help pay for her mom's hospital bills. "What can I do to make folks feel more at ease with selecting the vacant shop?"

"Max needs to solve this murder case pronto, so folks can have something else to talk about." Sander gave Lucy a significant look. "He probably could use some help." The mayor was asking for help from

Faye Investigations without technically asking for it. In other words, a pro bono case.

Since Lucy had planned to help clear Damien's name, it didn't make much of a difference to wade in deeper. Besides, her cousin had been chomping at the bit to jump full-tilt into the investigation. She gave a salute worthy of her foster grandma. "Aye, aye, Captain."

"I hope you'll keep me informed during your investigation."

"Isn't that the police chief's job?"

"I will ask him as well, my dear. But between the two of us, I have more faith in the reputation of Faye Investigations than a former assistant DA."

"Then why did you hire Max?" Lucy blurted out.

"He was the only person to meet all the qualifications, and the Board likes him." Sander shrugged. "He's a hard worker, but when it comes to murder, we can't compare him to an old pro like Stella."

Lucy bit the inside of her cheek to keep from laughing. What had Stella been telling the mayor? Since her cousin got her PI license decades ago, she had never actively participated in a case. And watching *CSI* didn't count.

"If we're not discussing the lease, why am I at this meeting?" Lucy asked, letting the confusion creep into her voice. Though she was disappointed, she wanted to be a good sport in case the lease was still on the table.

"Calla Louie wants the Monkey King statuette returned to the Chinese community. Since you found the artifact, I thought you could talk to her about why you didn't contest the town's ownership of it. After all, it was found on town property."

Lucy's mind whirled. While she wasn't a politician, this smelled of political doublespeak. Was she here because she was half Chinese? Was she here to convince Calla to give up the claim to the artifact? Or was she here doing public outreach work for free?

Knock! Knock!

Abby stuck her head into the room. "Are you ready to start the meeting, Mayor?"

Sander nodded. His wife held open the door. Calla Louie stepped through and crossed the room to take the seat next to Lucy.

Like most Asian women, Calla looked as if she could be in her thirties or forties, or maybe even in her fifties with an excellent skincare regimen. She was a slip of a woman, probably one hundred and ten pounds wet and tiny enough to make Lucy feel like a lumbering oaf next to her. Her black hair was chin-length with straight bangs. When she spoke, her voice was melodious and calm.

Abby closed the door and joined them, standing

slightly to the right of Sander's desk and holding a notepad.

During the brief introduction, Calla gave Lucy a curious glance and promptly ignored her. She reached into her purse and pulled out several sheets of stapled paper. "Mayor, this is a petition from the Chinese community, asking for the Monkey King artifact to be donated to our Chinese temple. The Monkey King is a significant mythical deity, and the artifact belongs to our people, not to be displayed for tourists."

Sander took the sheets of paper, leafed through them, and set it on his desk. "Miss Louie, you're asking the town to donate a significant amount of money to your temple. A university appraised the artifact at a quarter-million dollars. The town can't give away public funds to any nonprofit that asks for it."

"We're not asking for money, and the artifact doesn't belong to the town," Calla said, leaning forward in her seat. "It came from the early Chinese laborers who built the railroad. We're just asking for our belonging back."

Sander flicked a glance at Lucy, silently pleading with her.

Lucy leaned back on her seat. She wasn't getting in the middle of this discussion. It didn't matter if the artifact was brought over during the railroad days or if it came from a pirate ship, but she wasn't going against the town's Chinese community.

When Lucy was growing up, the Chinese population lived outside of the town proper, and their children went to a different school. She didn't interact with any of them in her youth. Now that she discovered the community, she wanted to know more about them.

Sander turned to Lucy. "What do you think?"

Lucy blinked. "I'm sorry, but I was woolgathering. Can you repeat the question?"

Calla addressed Lucy for the first time in Cantonese. "Santa Claus thinks we would be satisfied with setting up the exhibit for the artifact."

Lucy grimaced inwardly at the brisk tone. She flicked a glance at Sander. If they didn't resolve this amicably, she had a feeling there might be a court battle in the future.

"Maybe we should look at the temple before we make any decisions." Lucy glanced at Calla. "Would the community be open to having tourists visit the Chinese temple? After all, the Vatican offers tours to visitors." She used the comparison to the Vatican on purpose, hoping to flatter Calla.

Lucy didn't want to lose the museum's lease, but incorporating the Chinese Temple in their tourist map of the town might be a good idea. And this would give her a chance to check out the Chinese community.

Sander beamed at Lucy. "All right, I guess we're settled."

Calla scowled at the mayor. "Not so fast—"

"Mr. Mayor," Abby said, glancing down at her notebook. Your next appointment will be here any minute now. Do you want me to go downstairs with these ladies to bring him in?"

Calla's hands gripped the armrest of her chair. "The artifact belongs—"

"That sounds like a fine idea, Abby," the mayor said, jumping up from his seat. "This will give me just enough time to take care of business." He dashed out of the room before Calla even got a chance to get up from her chair.

"The call of nature?" Lucy said.

Calla snorted in disgust. She reached into her purse and pulled out a business card. "Here's my number. The ideal location for the artifact is in the temple."

Lucy sighed, scribbled her cell phone number onto a receipt, and handed it to Calla. She felt like the moss between two boulders. She didn't sign up for this.

Calla stomped out of the room.

"Are you okay, my dear?" Abby asked. The brown

eyes behind the wispy mud-brown bangs held curiosity rather than concern.

"I felt like the two of them just ran over me several times."

Abby chuckled. When she smiled, it smoothed all the angles on her face. Though she still didn't look like a jolly Mrs. Claus, she certainly looked friendlier. "It's always like that between the two of them. Calla tries to corner Sander, and he wiggles free one way or another."

An image of Santa Claus running away from an elf rose up in Lucy's mind, and she almost laughed. "This happens often?"

"All the time. Calla is Ah Louie's great-great-granddaughter." Abby said this statement as if it explained everything. "She is at all the city council meetings, making sure we consider the Chinese community's interest."

"I heard of Ah Louie several times growing up, but I don't know who he is."

"We'll have a small exhibit on Ah Louie. He was the leader who brought over the Chinese laborers for the railroads in this area back then. And when they were done building the railroad, Ah Louie opened up one of the most successful brickyards in the region. Almost all the red bricks in town came from his factory."

Lucy cocked her head, taking in the history

lesson. How come she didn't know anything about this? It didn't help that her father wasn't a local. Maybe this was why she never integrated with the Chinese community in town. "Does this include the red bricks in the tunnel system under the town?"

"How do you know about the tunnel system?" Abby asked, giving Lucy a sharp look.

Lucy shrugged. Her many times great-grandfather on her mother's side was one of the town's founding members and a pirate to boot. The Fayes even had access to it from underneath the PI office, but she wasn't sharing this with Abby. The city council had wanted the tunnels to be kept a secret since her grandfather's childhood. "Stories I heard from my grandfather."

"The city council doesn't want the public to know about the tunnel system," Abby said. "It isn't mapped, and we don't know their condition. We don't want folks, especially children, to wander around in there."

Lucy nodded to acknowledge Abby's words. Her grandfather had a set of maps for the tunnels. And from what she recalled of her childhood explorations, they were in pretty good shape. "Did you know Jason Albright? The man who was found in the vacant shop and later died in the hospital?" If Abby helped out routinely in City Hall, she must know most of the town employees.

Abby blinked at this change in topic. She nodded slowly. "I was acquainted with him."

"I heard he was planning to steal the artifact and sell it on the black market."

Abby stared at Lucy for a long moment. "Where did you hear this rumor?"

Lucy couldn't very well toss out Damien's name. "Someone made an offhand comment on the town's online message board. Was Jason the type who would do something like this?" She blinked innocently like she was chatting with a girlfriend at the coffee shop.

Abby smoothed her oversized sheath dress, avoiding Lucy's gaze. "Why are you asking me?"

"I find it odd that he was fired from the state, but he got a job quickly with the town," Lucy said. Steady employment in a small town was a valuable commodity. And a job with a pension would have applicants lining up a mile long.

A bead of sweat popped up at Abby's temple. "You'll have to ask the HR department. They do the hiring." She glanced at her watch. "I have to get going. The mayor's next meeting is about to start."

Abby ushered Lucy out of the room and out a side door that led to the public area. She closed the door behind Lucy, shutting the mayor's office from the general public.

Lucy stood there for a long moment, staring at

the shadow moving behind the frosted glass insert on the door. She could put in a public information request, but there might be a confidentiality policy that would only allow them to acknowledge his employment. But from Abby's reaction to Lucy's questions, someone high up must have given Jason the job. Someone like the mayor? Had Jason blackmailed Sander? And did Abby know about it?

10

SWEET TASTE OF LOVE

The next morning, Lucy woke with the taste of fur in her mouth. Yuck! She spat it out and swiped her mouth with an arm.

Raspberry yowled next to her ear. Not a gentle meow, but a full-on cat-in-pain screech.

Lucy jerked fully awake and sneezed several times. Her eyes itched like there was sand in them. When was the last time she took her allergy medicine? With Raspberry prowling in her bed, Lucy would have to wash the sheets. There was probably enough cat dander to constrict her airways and kill her in the middle of the night.

"What are you doing in here, Little Emperor?" Lucy said. Normally, her sister's cat slept downstairs, far away from Lucy.

Raspberry ignored her and sat down on her pillow, rubbing his privates into her silk pillowcase.

"Oh, gross," Lucy said, fully awake by now. "The silk sheet set was a gift from my grandma for my thirty-ninth birthday," Lucy said.

The cat spread his legs and licked himself.

Lucy turned her head. This was not the image she wanted in her head first thing in the morning. It was pretty obvious that Raspberry wanted his breakfast, and he wanted it now, just like a Little Emperor.

A few minutes later, Lucy was in the kitchen, adding food to the pet bowl and changing the water. Raspberry sat on his hindquarters, watching her through slitted eyes with an imperial tilt to his chin.

Lucy sighed. At least he wasn't yowling or trying to trip her by trailing after her. At close to thirty-five pounds, the Main Coon could take her down any time he wished.

She grabbed her keys. Coffee and a pastry from the Shoreline Café were much more appealing than a peanut butter and jelly sandwich. "Be a good boy, Raspberry. Your auntie is off to visit Grandma and to do some more sleuthing." She waited, hoping for a warm response from the animal.

Raspberry buried his face in his food and ignored her—typical male.

Lucy checked to make sure the pet door was open and left the house. At the bakery, she ordered two lattes and two bear claws. Nurse Bobbi deserved time off after finding Jason Albright's body, but a treat was probably the closest thing she would get.

The two-story 1950s hospital building looked much like it did before Jason's death. There was no extra security or police patrol on the premises. Not that Lucy expected any increase in security now that the victim was dead.

As Lucy's boots clicked on the tile floor and her eyes adjusted to the fluorescent overhead lights, she wondered for the first time if she should stop coming by every morning. The doctors had said her mother could hear her, but after weeks of a one-way monologue detailing all of Lucy's resentment and hurt feelings from her childhood, she was done.

And as she gazed at her mother, week after week, Lucy realized that life was too short to hold on to her past like it was a badge of honor. The past was the past, and it was time to let it go. More than anything else, she wanted to feel her mother's arms around her again.

At the nurses' station, Lucy greeted Nurse Bobbi. She held out a coffee cup and the white pastry bag. "I got you breakfast. How are you holding up? I'm surprised you're back at work so soon."

Nurse Bobbi accepted the goodies and thanked Lucy. "I have to be. I'm a single mother, and I need to save my vacation leave for my child."

"You are amazing. I don't know how you do it on your own."

Nurse Bobbi shrugged, turning pink at the cheeks. "I didn't think I could do it either, but you just do. I am lucky that I have my mother around to help me out once in a while. She is still working too, so I can't rely on her all the time."

"If you ever get yourself into a jam, there's always me. I don't have any experience with kids, but yours is old enough that an endless supply of *Curious George* videos and a peanut butter and jelly sandwich should do the trick."

Nurse Bobbi jumped up from her seat and came around the counter to give Lucy a quick hug. "You can't imagine how much the offer means to me."

Lucy knew very well what she was offering. Her mother had been in a similar situation as a single working parent. While her dad wasn't a deadbeat, he had lived out of town and only came in once a month to spend time with her. This wasn't much help for those times when her mother needed last-minute childcare for emergencies.

The two of them munched on their pastries and shared chitchat for several minutes.

Nurse Bobbi's cell phone buzzed, and she glanced at the screen. "I better get going. Time for me to make my rounds."

Lucy asked casually, "Have the police finished processing the crime scene?"

Nurse Bobbi gave her a sharp look. "Oh, don't use that tone on me. Why are you looking into the Chicken Man's death?"

"His name is Jason Albright. We can stop calling him the Chicken Man. As for why I'm looking into it, I have several reasons. First, if we can solve the case, we can use it as an advertisement that our services haven't changed under the new management. Second, the mayor doesn't want to discuss the lease for the new museum until this murder is a faint memory."

Lucy left Damien's involvement out of the conversation on purpose. For some reason, she still felt protective of his privacy. When she had time, she would have to examine these feelings. She hoped they weren't the beginnings of a romantic interest. The last thing she needed was a boyfriend.

Nurse Bobbi gave Lucy a cheeky smile. "And this is hush-hush because Max doesn't want you looking into it."

"Max doesn't tell me what to do. Besides, if the real killer gets wind of this, both you and I could be in trouble. "

"Me? I don't know anything."

"You found Jason's body, and you were his nurse.

The killer could think you know more than you actually know."

Nurse Bobbi shuddered. "I can't get involved in this. I'm a single mom. What will happen to my girl if something happens to me?"

Lucy patted Nurse Bobbi's hand, ignoring the quick stab of guilt. The nurse was probably safe enough, but Lucy needed to push her to get information. "Why don't you tell me what you know. When Jason was brought in, was he poisoned?"

"I can't tell you. Patient confidentiality."

"I don't think Jason cares one way or the other what you tell me."

Nurse Bobbi considered Lucy's words for a long moment. "You're probably right. What does it matter now? Someone put antifreeze in his iced tea."

"Wouldn't he be able to tell from the first sip that there was something off about his drink?"

"That's the problem. Antifreeze has a sweet taste to it, so the sweetened iced tea probably masked it."

"And the symptoms were slurred words and loss of coordination? I thought he was drunk when he stumbled out of the vacant shop," Lucy said.

"He was lucky that you were at the shop. The doctor pumped his stomach before the antifreeze metabolized further into his system and caused organ failure. If not for...I don't even know what to call it...the hanging, we could have saved him."

"That part is what my foster grandma would call fate. There's nothing we can do to help him escape it," Lucy said.

And by all accounts, his shady personality and business dealings might have had something to do with it. After all, he must have made someone really angry or desperate to put out an assassination contract for him on the dark web.

"I can't believe the killer was bold enough to come to the hospital for a second attempt," Nurse Bobbi said.

"I'm assuming Jason was killed shortly after the nurses made their last round. What time would that be?"

"We checked in on Jason every two hours, but he wasn't killed during the night. He was killed sometime in the morning. When I did my first round at eight o'clock, he was still alive."

Lucy blinked. For some reason, she had assumed Jason was killed overnight, and his body was discovered in the morning. "I don't remember the exact time when I got here that particular morning. But I usually get here between nine thirty and ten to see my mom. So he was killed sometime between eight and ten."

Nurse Bobbi nodded. "That sounds about right. We just started visiting hours."

Lucy frowned. She never had to sign in when she

visited her mom, so there was probably no visitor log. "Do you remember any of the other visitors?"

"I was too busy to pay any attention. We were getting ready for the mayor's visit," Nurse Bobbi said.

It must have been an official visit if the staff had to make preparations. "Why was Sander visiting the hospital?" Lucy asked.

"For the ribbon-cutting of the remodeled children's wing. I didn't think he would visit this wing afterward, but my supervisor wanted us to spruce up the place anyway, just in case."

"What time was the ribbon cutting?"

"At nine."

"And did he come by here afterward?"

"Of course not. By that time, we'd discovered Jason's body, and the police taped off this section."

Lucy felt a quick flash of relief. Folks would notice Sander's absence before the ribbon-cutting, so he couldn't have finished off Jason. "Who else was part of his entourage? For an event like this, he probably had several people with him."

"I don't know. I wasn't in the area."

"I can't ask who attended the ribbon-cutting without raising some eyebrows. Do you think you can ask for me?" Lucy said, holding her breath.

Nurse Bobbi chewed her lower lip for a while. "How about this—I can ask to see the photographs some of the girls took of the event."

Lucy nodded. "Sounds great. And I will check on the hospital's social media profiles to see what photographs were put up for the ribbon-cutting ceremony. One way or another, I think we can piece together who was at the event from the mayor's office."

LUCY LEFT THE NURSES' station and made her way to her mother's room. As she stepped into the room, the noise from the hallway disappeared. Her attention was on the whirring and beeping machines that kept her mother alive.

She sat with a sigh. With each passing day, Lucy's hope for her mother's recovery diminished. Coming here every morning was getting old, and it wore on her. Maybe it was time to get on with her life.

She reached for her mother's hand. "Hi, Mom. It's Lucy again. If you can hear me, please move your hand."

A second passed and then another. Lucy opened her mouth to speak again when Mom's index finger twitched.

Lucy's eyes widened, and she stared at her hand with a laser focus. "Mom, did you just move your hand? Please move it again for me." Her voice was thick with emotion.

Don't get your hopes up, said a small voice in the back of her head.

Lucy held her breath.

Nothing. No movement at all.

Lucy sat back in her chair, breaking contact with her mom. She swiped a hand across her face and brushed the tears coming out of her eyes. "Mom, I can't do this anymore. I just can't. I am so sorry." She stared into her mother's face, hoping for any response.

There was none. The seconds ticked away, along with Lucy's hope.

Lucy swallowed the lump in her throat. This was not the time to feel sorry for herself. She had things to do, and people to take care of. Without hope, she wasn't sure how she could fill the hole in her heart.

Knock! Knock!

Lucy dragged her gaze from her mother to glance at the doorway.

Nurse Bobbi stood at the threshold. "Hon, the police chief wants to talk to you. He's waiting for you at the nurses' station."

"Is it possible my mom is awake? I thought I felt her hand move," Lucy said. She cringed at the pleading note in her voice.

Nurse Bobbi glanced at Dahlia and back to Lucy. "Did she do it more than once?"

Lucy hung her head, disappointment settling into the pit of her stomach. "No."

"I'm sorry. It was probably muscle spasms. It happens sometimes."

Lucy exhaled and stood. "I better go talk to Max."

"Don't worry, hon. I'll take good care of your mom."

Lucy left the room without a backward glance. She was glad Nurse Bobbi interrupted her. Another second alone with Mom would reduce her to a wailing mess.

As she strolled to the nurses' station at the center of the hall, she straightened her shoulders and wiped at her face one more time. She could see Max leaning against the countertop and flipping through his notebook. The act was probably more for show than anything else. He had the uncanny ability to recall everything said to him without notes.

At Lucy's approaching footsteps, Max glanced up from his notebook. He tucked it inside his jacket pocket. His moss-green eyes peered at her face with concern. "Lucy, are you okay? Is this a good time to talk?"

Lucy nodded. "It's as good as any other time. You want to do it here?"

"You had lunch yet? The sandwiches from the hospital cafeteria aren't bad, but you might want to avoid the coffee."

Lucy gave him a half-smile at his attempt to cheer her up.

They strolled over to the elevator and went downstairs to the cafeteria without small talk. Max seemed to sense that Lucy needed the time to get her feelings under control.

11

OCEAN'S ELEVEN

Lucy picked up a tray and got in line at the food counter. The scent of fresh bread, smoked meat, and burned coffee sent her stomach into a joyful flurry. She ordered an unsweetened iced tea and a Cobb salad—with extra bread—even though she would love nothing better than a roast beef sandwich with oozing melted cheese. Getting back into her jeans was too important, and she didn't like Jane Fonda well enough for a long-term relationship. Those VHS exercise tapes were only a means to an end.

Though the cafeteria still had the 1950s black-and-white checkered tile floor, the remodeled decor was more desperate than trendy. The accent wall was a pale green with words like "fresh" and "local" stamped in a random pattern. The wrought iron bistro tables and chairs could have belonged to a Parisian cafe but looked uninviting under the harsh fluorescent light. The piped-in music sounded like elevator music, more annoying than relaxing.

Lucy and Max found a table in a corner, far enough away from the other diners. For the first ten minutes, they ate in silence. Max chewed on his chicken marinara sandwich with the kind of gusto that made Lucy envious. She nibbled on the bacon bits and pushed the lettuce around her plate.

Max wiped a napkin over his face and sat back in his chair. "Officer Martinez mentioned you thought Damien North searched Jason Albright before he collapsed in the parking lot. Can you tell me what happened?"

Lucy reached for the glass of water and took a slow sip, dragging the moment out. How much should she tell him? Was this the moment when she had to pick a side? And what exactly was she picking?

"I was on the curb, talking to the mayor before he left," Lucy said. "From my angle behind Damien, I thought he huddled over Jason's body because he was performing CPR. Then he reached for the knapsack and let the chicken out. But Stella was in the PI office, looking out into the parking lot while she spoke to the dispatcher. From her angle, she saw Damien searching Jason's pockets."

"Why didn't you tell me this before Jason's death? Or did you and Stella withhold information to protect Damien?"

"It was secondhand information. I didn't know about it until Stella told me later. And for all I knew, she could have mistaken the entire thing."

"It's not just omitting a minor detail, Lucy. I didn't even know Damien North was at the scene until you mentioned this detail to Officer Martinez. Do you know how suspicious it is for the town reporter to disappear during a headline story?"

Lucy gave him an apologetic smile. "Well, now you know. It's not too late to question Damien."

"If I can find him. No one has seen him for days."

"I spoke to him yesterday at the lighthouse. He has been camping in a sea cave all this time." Lucy hoped Damien didn't have an accident on the wet slippery rocks. Maybe she should have offered to help him pack up. "Last I heard, he was returning home."

"Do you know which sea cave?"

Lucy shook her head. "I didn't think to ask."

"What did the two of you talk about?"

"Damien asked how Jason was doing. He didn't know that Jason had died at the hospital."

"How did he react to the news?"

"He was shocked, and..." Lucy hesitated. Was it

normal for Damien to automatically assume he was a suspect?

Max raised an eyebrow, daring her to lie.

Lucy winced inwardly. She didn't want Max to accuse her of picking Damien over him. Both of their friendships were equally important to her. "And he thinks he's a murder suspect."

"Shouldn't you think the same? First, Damien searched through Jason Albright's pockets and disappeared even though it's his job to report on the story. Second, he went into hiding and didn't reappear again until after Jason's death. Don't you find this behavior suspicious?"

"Since you put it that way, yes. At the time, I didn't know to be suspicious," Lucy said, all of which was true.

"You can become an accessory to murder. Is this what you want?" There was a hint of anger in Max's tone.

Lucy's eyes widened. This had actually never occurred to her. "No! I had nothing to do with Jason Albright's death. And I don't think Damien has anything to do with it either."

"Then why did he go into hiding?"

"Damien thought Jason was stalking him." Lucy explained Jason's idea of stealing the Monkey King statuette to sell in the black market. She left out the part about Damien's eccentric rich uncle. It would only complicate things. "That's why Damien was avoiding Jason. He wanted nothing to do with the scheme."

Max shook his head. "Didn't you wonder why Jason thought Damien would be interested in the scheme?"

Lucy shrugged. "Maybe Damien has a skill that Jason lacked." *Like bringing in the buyer*, she said to herself.

Max considered her words and nodded slowly. "Like *Ocean's Eleven* or *The Italian Job*? Maybe Jason was recruiting a gang for the heist."

"Whoa. I think you're going down the wrong path here. For all we know, the gang might just be Jason." She held up one finger. "One person. Maybe the plan to steal the artifact died with Jason."

"Or maybe there was an argument among the gang members, and they had to silence Jason."

"Our small town doesn't have the kind of sophisticated technology that would require a specialized gang of thieves. The artifact is in the vault at the Community Bank, which only has three security cameras."

Max narrowed his eyes. "How do you know the camera count at the bank? Are you part of this gang?"

Lucy gave Max a deadpan stare. "I counted them the last time I was there to withdraw cash."

"Sorry, but I had to ask the question. Now back to my idea. You'd need someone to disable the cameras, someone to crack the vault, and someone familiar with the routine at the bank. And don't forget about the getaway driver. That's at least four people already."

Lucy gaped at him. This theory sounded more like a plot for Hollywood. Sometimes she wondered if Max's upbringing in Southern California made him more susceptible to harebrained ideas.

"The statuette isn't even worth that much money," she said. "If someone wants it that badly, they can go down to the bank with a note and a gun. There's no need for such an elaborate scheme. This is not the movies."

Max crossed his arms. "You have your theory, and I have mine. Who else would want to kill Jason?"

Lucy wondered if Max was purposely pumping her for information by being this obtuse. "I don't know. The person who paid an assassin over the dark web to kill Jason? Or maybe his wife? They say most of the time it's the spouse. Maybe she got sick and tired of nagging him to take out the trash."

She sounded flippant, but she was annoyed with Max. Was he trying to pin this crime on Damien?

Max ignored her tone. "How did you find out

about this assassin? Was there an attempt previously?"

"Rosalynn Albright told me about it." Lucy explained the assassination market scam.

"If an FBI agent took this supposed assassination contract seriously, he would notify the local police so we could follow up with Jason. I wonder if he made up the story."

"Come on. It's too far-fetched to be made up. Why would Jason make up such a story? Most people don't even understand blockchain technology and crypto-currency."

"Maybe Jason is hiding his tracks. This way he could disappear to organize the heist without his wife being suspicious."

Lucy rubbed her temple. Were they back to the heist theory again? "The Albrights have been separated for a while. I don't think she would have cared if he went into hiding."

"Then he probably made the whole thing up to get her attention. Rosalynn was the one who left him, not the other way around. Maybe he wanted her back."

Lucy paused, recalling her conversation with Rosalynn Albright. She had spoken the proper words to hint at sadness, but there was a tinge of happiness in her bearing. She was technically the widow who would inherit his assets. Heck, she probably had a stronger motive to kill him than anyone else.

Max glanced at his half-eaten sandwich. "I better get a doggy bag for this and finish it in the office. I need to call the FBI and track down Rosalynn." He glanced at the salad on Lucy's plate. "Do you want to take that home?"

Lucy shook her head and shoved another bite of salad in her mouth. She was being good, but she wasn't a saint. No way was she planning to finish the salad with the cheat meal tonight.

As Max returned to the food counter, she finished her unsweetened tea and went back to the drink fountain to get a refill. By the time she came back to the table, he had already wrapped his sandwich in plain white waxed paper.

Lucy paused, reaching out to touch the paper.

Max gave her a puzzled look. "I know you're not a rabbit girl, so if you want it, I can get something else from the drive-through on the way back. You don't have to try to impress me. I like a woman with curves."

Lucy gave him a sideways glance and snorted. Should she bust his bubble or let him have his moment of vanity? "What does the fit of my jeans have to do with you?"

Max blushed.

"Seriously, it is so not about you." She set the

fountain drink cup down next to the wrapped sand-wich and unwrapped his sandwich. "Does this look familiar?"

Max glanced at the half-eaten sandwich on plain white waxed paper and the fountain drink cup. His jaw dropped. "Jason's poisoned iced tea came from here."

Lucy should probably mention that Rosalynn worked at the billing department somewhere in the building, but she was still annoyed with Max over the heist theory. Besides, she wanted to renew her friendship with her childhood friend before trouble came calling on the new widow.

12

CHANNELING PO PO

During the drive back to the PI office, Lucy reviewed the conversation with Max. She wasn't sure why she was irritated with him. What if he became too caught up in this heist theory and missed the clues leading to the murderer?

Or maybe she was mad at herself for listening to Stella and omitting the details about Damien's involvement. If Lucy had listened to her gut instinct, she wouldn't feel out of sorts about the situation. Hopefully, everything would resolve itself once Max talked to Damien.

The next few hours flew by in a blur of activities. Lucy made several phone calls that had more to do with her marketing work for the local businesses than any actual investigation. Creating a website for the yarn shop was a lot harder than she initially thought. Why would someone buy online from Tammy next door when the big box stores offered better pricing? Lucy called a cleaning company to take care of the vacant shop and got an appointment for later in the week.

By the time Stella wandered into the inner office, asking about dinner, Lucy was ready to call it quits for the day. It was much easier working a nine-to-five job than piecemealing gigs for multiple bosses. Lucy shut down her computer. Time enough to think about it tomorrow.

"Where do the locals go to eat and gossip?" Lucy asked. She hoped it wasn't a seedy dive bar. "We can listen in on some conversations."

"I know just the place," Stella said. "We can go to Fisherman's Catch. It's a little hole in the wall seafood bar off the pier. It gets all the leftover catch of the day that didn't make it to the other restaurants or the fish market. The tourists like the fancier Sea King and its view of the ocean, but you can feed an entire family at Fisherman's Catch for the same cost."

The Sea King was a turn-of-the-century steamboat that used to shuttle goods up and down the Sacramento River but later made its way to the coast at Morro Cliff. The new owner converted the steamboat to a fine dining restaurant, which revitalized the pier area and drove up the prices.

The Fisherman's Catch wasn't even on the pier. It was a good five blocks behind the City Hall on a patch of dirt with overgrown weeds. The gravel parking lot was full, and Lucy ended up parking a block away. When Stella had said the Fisherman's Catch was a hole in the wall, she had meant it.

The old-fashioned plywood sign was faded and unlit, making it hard to spot in the fading purple dusk. Yellow light spilled out from circular windows designed to look like portholes on a ship. Even before Lucy stepped in through the heavy double wooden doors, the heavy scent of deep-fried fish and grease wafted out to greet her. It was her kind of place.

Stella ordered the grilled sea bass with wild rice and zucchini. Lucy got the beer-battered cod fish and chips with a side of clam chowder soup. Her mouth watered, and her stomach danced a jig. Now this was real food, not that wimpy salad she had for lunch.

They grabbed their number table marker and found a table in a corner. The walls were wood paneled with exposed beams. Nautical ship steering wheels, messages in murky bottles, treasure chests, and netting were scattered throughout the restaurant.

With the dim light and the general hubbub of conversation around them, Lucy hoped they could chat freely without worrying about eavesdroppers. She told Stella about her conversations with Rosalynn, Sander, and Max.

"I can't believe Max is stuck on the theory that Jason is recruiting for a Hollywood-style heist," Lucy said. "It is utterly ridiculous."

"Are you sure that's how Max really reacted? I know he's a little green, but this almost sounds like he's lost his marbles," Stella said.

"You think he's laying it on a little too thick, being the bumbling small-town cop?" Lucy said.

Stella nodded. "Exactly. I think he's baiting you."

Lucy was taken aback. "Why?"

"He probably needs help, but he can't ask you for it. At least not directly. After all, he is a man. And he's at that stage in your"—she made air quotes with her fingers—"friendship where he's still trying to impress you."

"He wants me to help solve Jason Albright's murder?" It sounded a little too far-fetched to Lucy. Green or not, cops didn't ask civilians to help them solve their cases.

Stella leaned forward with the gleam in her eye. "I'm sure of it. Don't forget, Lulu, he's an outsider, and he's only been in town for a few months. Folks don't talk to him like he's a neighbor. But you're one of us. Even though you haven't been around much, the Faye name can open a lot of doors in our community."

Lucy considered Stella's words. Maybe her cousin was right. Look at how easily Rosalynn Albright had chatted, even though they hadn't seen each other since they were teens.

"In that case, maybe I should have applied for the police chief job." Lucy smiled to show that she was joking. She didn't have the qualifications or the inclination for such a position. Who wanted to work around the clock on a small government salary? If she was going to work around the clock like that, she was better off being her own boss.

Stella sat back with a thoughtful look. "Now that's an idea. I wonder if it could be done."

Lucy rolled her eyes. "I was only kidding."

Stella shrugged nonchalantly. "Hey, we're a small hick town. We do whatever we want out here. Isn't that what they say in the big city?" There was a hint of wistfulness in her voice.

"You ever thought about moving away? You don't need to stay here anymore, now that your parents are gone."

"Can't. I gotta take care of your mom now."

Lucy gaped at Stella. Her cousin practically volunteered to be her mom's caretaker, which meant Lucy was off the hook. If she left for San

Francisco, Stella probably wouldn't blame her for leaving.

A lump rose in her throat, and she swallowed it. First, the uncle that took Lucy in as a runaway teen. And now, a cousin who was practically her older sister. What did she do in her previous life to deserve this good fortune?

Lucy reached across the table and squeezed Stella's hand. "Then I guess I'll have to keep you company for a while."

Stella beamed at her. "And to quote your foster grandma—we single ladies gotta make some noise."

A server appeared next to their table and slid their plates onto the table and left. Lucy blinked at the efficiency. He didn't even waste effort on making eye contact. Obviously, he wasn't working for tips.

Stella picked up her fork. "This place isn't known for service, but the food is amazing." She popped a bite of sea bass into her mouth.

Lucy broke off a piece of the battered cod and dipped it into the tartar sauce. Crispy on the outside and soft on the inside. The creamy and tangy tartar sauce was the perfect condiment. The soup had a bite of chewy clam in every spoonful. The creamy flavor blended with the clam juice and just a hint of onion, garlic, and thyme. She sighed in satisfaction. This was heaven. The best meal she'd had since leaving San Francisco and its numerous tasty takeout options.

"I can't have fish and chips anywhere else after this meal," Lucy said, pausing for air.

"Do you always eat like this?" Stella said.

Lucy glanced up from her food. "What?"

"You were making this noise the entire time you were eating. It was a cross between a hum and a moan. I'm surprised you weren't swaying side to side."

Lucy flushed. Was she really doing that? "You know I don't cook. I haven't had anything this good in weeks. How come you didn't take me here sooner?"

"You don't cook? What do you do for your meals?"

"In San Francisco, I go out to eat with friends or I get takeout on the way home from work. Sometimes I stop by the Wong family restaurant for free food."

"What about since you came back here?"

Lucy shrugged, even more embarrassed at the astonishment in Stella's voice. "I rotate between peanut butter and jelly sandwiches, spaghetti, and canned chili."

"Oh, you poor thing. If I'd known this, I would have invited you over for dinner more often. I'm not much of a cook, but I love to bake. We can have dessert every night."

Lucy grinned. Dessert every night sounded wonderful, especially when made by someone else. "Unfortunately, I have to turn you down. I don't have the Faye metabolism. I have to work pretty hard just to look like this." She gestured at the extra twenty pounds on her body. "Dad died from a heart attack, and I am not going down that path."

"I know—we should enroll in a cooking class together," Stella said with a beaming smile.

The smile stayed on Lucy's face, but she probably looked more like a wax doll now. "No, thank you. My first priority is getting a private investigator license."

Stella sat back in her chair, deflated. It was pretty obvious she wanted a bestie.

As much as Lucy liked and appreciated Stella, Lucy wasn't looking for someone glued to her hip.

"What about the Silver Fox?" Lucy said. "Maybe he would be interested in taking some classes with you?"

"I can't ask him. I was hoping to impress him with my new skills."

Lucy chuckled and glanced around the restaurant for the first time. When her gaze landed on a couple at the table kitty corner from them, she blinked.

Rosalynn Albright smiled at the man seated across from her. She stroked his face, but he grabbed her hand and kissed her palm. She laughed at him.

Lucy dragged her gaze back to her food. Holy Toledo! Rosalynn had more than one motive for getting rid of her husband. First, she would inherit his assets. And now, she just made room for another man in her life.

Stella began twisting around and looked over her shoulder. "What are you staring at?"

"Don't turn around."

Stella froze and shifted her gaze back at Lucy. "Okay." With her body half twisted to the side, she looked uncomfortable. She slowly turned until she faced Lucy again. "Better?"

Lucy flicked a glance over Stella's shoulder. The couple in the corner weren't even paying attention to them. "It's Rosalynn Albright. She's making kissy faces with a man."

"Is she now?" Stella gave Lucy a significant look. "Do we have our first suspect?"

Lucy nodded. "It seems Rosalynn has more than one motive for wanting her husband dead." She told Stella about Rosalynn working in the billing department at the hospital. "This means she has both the motive and the opportunity. I need to talk to the billing department about mom's bills, so I'll drop by and ask her co-workers some questions tomorrow."

"Who else is on your suspect list?"

Lucy lowered her voice. "Sander Frasier. He could have been blackmailed into giving Jason a job. And he was at the ribbon-cutting ceremony at the hospital that morning."

Stella looked taken back. "Sander? No way. He's our year-round Santa Claus. He has been mayor since forever. He's the biggest champion for our town, trying to improve tourism and creating more local jobs. I don't believe it. Lots of people won't believe it."

"If Jason Albright was blackmailing Sander, the mayor might have to resort to murder to get rid of Jason."

"But Sander is one of the good guys. What could he have done that needed the silence of a grave?"

"He's a politician. I'm sure there's dirt some-where. I wish I could talk to him without his wife in the room."

"Abby needs a hobby. Now that their son is grown, she 'volunteers' her time at City Hall. If I were in her shoes, I wouldn't want to see my husband twenty-four seven."

Lucy considered Stella's words. It was a strange arrangement. Was Abby helping out or monitoring her husband's activities? Did this mean... "Have there been any whispers of Sander with another woman?"

"Of course not. He's a good family man." Stella

waved a hand dismissively. "I guess folks might suspect the two of us, but we grew up together. Our parents were neighbors, so I have always known Sander. He's like a brother to me."

Lucy raised an eyebrow. "What if Abby doesn't see your friendship with her husband this way?"

"What are you trying to say?"

"I'm not sure." Lucy ignored her unease and filled Stella in on the conversation she had at City Hall yesterday morning. "I'm not even sure what my role is in all this. Can I bill the mayor for my time?"

"Absolutely. Send him a bill. If he wants your marketing expertise to make this museum a success, then he should pay for it."

"I wonder if Abby was at the hospital during the ribbon-cutting ceremony? And unlike Sander, no one would care about Abby's every move," Lucy said.

Stella considered Lucy's words. "You might be onto something. All this time, we thought Jason had blackmailed Sander for a town job, but what if he blackmailed Abby instead?"

They were both silent for a long moment, considering Stella's comment.

Lucy thought back to the interaction between the mayor and his wife. "Do you know how Sander and Abby met? Their relationship felt strange, like it was more of a marriage of convenience than for love."

"Sander got Abby pregnant in high school, and they got married before their son was born. At first, Sander's family was against the marriage, but later on supported it. I don't know why they changed their minds."

"Why were they against the marriage?"

"Abby is from the trailer park, and his family owns a third of the town. He was supposed to go to Harvard that fall, but because of Abby, he ended up at a state university."

Lucy filed the information away. She needed to have a chat with Sander. His marriage sounded complicated, and it might also be his weakness, which might have opened him up for blackmail.

For the rest of the meal, Lucy kept an eye on Rosalynn's table. When her childhood friend headed toward the restroom, Lucy slapped a tip on the table. "Rosalynn is on the move. I'm going to get her to introduce me to her man."

Stella followed Rosalynn's progress with her gaze. "Go get her, Tiger."

"I need you to create a distraction so that I can talk to the boyfriend alone after the introduction."

"How do I do that?" Stella asked.

"I don't know. Channel your inner Po Po." Lucy's foster grandma could create a distraction or disaster just by opening her mouth. Lucy got up. "Get creative."

13

SECRET WEAPON

Lucy stepped into the restroom and gaped at the mermaid theme—murals of mermaids sunning on rocks, waving from the foamy sea, and frolicking with sailors on the beach. And of course, the buxom mermaids wore itty-bitty seashell bras. A man must have come up with the idea.

There was no one at the sinks, and only one stall was occupied. Lucy turned on the sink and took her time lathering up the liquid soap. The stall door opened from behind her, but Lucy kept her attention focused on her hands.

"Lucy?" Rosalynn asked. Her voice echoed in the space.

Lucy glanced at the mirror in front of her. She pretended to be surprised at seeing Rosalynn's reflection on it. "Rosalynn! I haven't seen you for decades, and now I see you everywhere. You aren't stalking me, are you?"

Rosalynn rolled her gray eyes and grinned. She wore a boat neck top that gathered at her thick waist. "You were always the funny one."

"Are you here by yourself? Do you want to get a drink together?" Lucy asked, knowing full well Rosalynn would have to turn her down.

Rosalynn shook her head, swinging her helmet of glossy black hair. "I'm here with my boyfriend." She blushed. "We have been dating for a year, long before Jason's death."

Lucy gave her a sideways glance. Now, why did Rosalynn feel like she had to explain herself? "Can I meet him? Or..." She trailed off, hoping it implied that there was something wrong with the guy.

"Yes! Of course, you can meet him. We are not hiding our relationship."

Lucy stepped away from the sink and grabbed a paper towel. Rosalynn's one-year relationship only made her appear fishier. If she had been in this relationship for a month or less, she could easily say the relationship was not serious, and she didn't need to kill Jason. As it was, she was still the prime suspect.

While Lucy dried her hands, Rosalynn washed hers.

"Do you come here often? This is my first time, and I love the food," Lucy said.

"At least once a week," Rosalynn said, drying her hands. "This is Marco's favorite restaurant. His mother doesn't cook fish, so he has to eat out to get his fix. Come on. Let me introduce you to him."

As Lucy followed Rosalynn to her table, she made a note of two facts. Marco's mother didn't cook fish, but this wouldn't matter if Marco had his own place. But needing to get his fish fix outside the home meant he was still living with his mother. A mama's boy or mama's caretaker?

Marco Domenico stood when Rosalynn and Lucy approached the table. The Italian man appeared to be in his early forties with dark brown hair. His temples were starting to gray. When he smiled, the corners of his warm hazel eyes crinkled adorably. And when he spoke, there was a slight hint of an accent that added to his distinguished gentleman vibe. But if his mother was still cooking and doing his laundry, he wasn't dateable as far as Lucy was concerned. Maybe Rosalynn liked the idea of being his mother's replacement.

Rosalynn made the introductions. Marco glanced politely at Lucy and said the right words, but his gaze didn't stray from Rosalynn. Oh, the man was in love, and it didn't take a genius to know it was an all-consuming love like the first time a teenager fell in love. Enough to kill someone's husband? He would have to be pretty desperate to do it, and he didn't seem like the type.

Lucy stood awkwardly next to the table, shifting from foot to foot, waiting for Stella's distraction.

Rosalynn and Marco shared a look. Before they could edge around Lucy, she blurted out, "How did the two of you meet?"

Marco's smile became fixed, losing its earlier warmth. "Babe, we should get—"

Rosalynn ignored him and launched into her story. They had met at the hospital cafeteria. "Marco is the hospital's IT contractor."

Lucy studied Marco from the corners of her eyes. With his background, wouldn't he know his way around the dark web? Did he hire someone to kill Jason using crypto-currency? Even with Lucy's limited knowledge, she knew the assassination market was a scam, so it wouldn't make sense for Marco to fall for it.

Was there more than one person who wanted to kill Jason? After all, there had been three different attempts at Jason's life—hiring an assassin, poisoning his iced tea, and finally strangling him with a sheet. Three different attempts by three different people? Or was there only one person responsible for all three attempts? This was food for thought. And it was giving her a headache.

A fire alarm blared. Lucy glanced around the

restaurant, trying to locate the source of the alarm. Smoke billowed out of the hallway that led to the restrooms. Half a heartbeat later, the sprinklers came on, drenching everyone and everything. Fabulous. Stella's distraction was clearing the restaurant. How was Lucy supposed to talk to Marco alone when he was in panic mode?

Marco grabbed his jacket and Rosalynn's hand. They joined the rest of the diners and workers rushing toward an exit. Lucy swiped at the wet hair dripping into her eyes. She sighed and marched out of the building. The next time Lucy talked to her foster grandma, she would ask Po Po to give Stella some sidekick training. Now Lucy would need an excuse to talk to Marco. Maybe she could break Stella's computer.

LUCY WOKE to find Raspberry clawing the throw pillows in the living room. The Little Emperor batted the stuffing around the room and pounced at imaginary shadows. He ignored Lucy like she was the furniture. No. He actually interacted with the furniture more than he did with her. She was invisible.

Lucy averted her eyes and made a beeline to the kitchen. Coffee first. Anger later. The Little Emperor would have to go. She was done cat sitting the ungrateful brat. Her sister would have to figure something out.

Raspberry followed Lucy into the kitchen, meowing sweetly like he could read her mind. He even rubbed up against her ankles with his chunky tushy. What a gigolo.

Lucy stared down at the cat in disgust. "It's a little too late, Little Emperor. I'm breaking up with you."

Raspberry kept rubbing her ankles and meowing like his heart was broken.

Lucy rolled her eyes and ignored the cat. She didn't have time to delve into cat psychology. As she made coffee and a PB&J sandwich, her thoughts drifted to Damien. It was time to check in on the reporter and see if he found any additional information on the murder case. He wasn't the type to sit idly while she had all the fun.

And later in the afternoon, she had a meeting with Calla Louie and Abby Frasier to tour the Chinese temple. The text message for the meeting came right before she'd climbed into bed last night. She'd almost declined, but she'd promised to help the mayor. Not only was the museum lease on the line, but future marketing work to help bring in tourism.

She refilled Raspberry's food and water bowls. "Little Emperor, your auntie is off to save the world. If you need to claw at something, find something outside. One more strike, and you're out of here."

And with that stern warning, she left the house. While she drove to the PI office, she munched on the PB&J sandwich. A few minutes later, she knocked at the door of the newspaper office. Through the windows, she saw Damien get up from his desk and unlock the door.

Lucy stepped inside and greeted Damien. "It's good to see you back in the swing of things. Do you have anything to report on Jason Albright's death?"

"Other than Max DeWitt harassing me?" Damien said in frustration. "Everywhere I turn, I see a cop tailing me. And no one will talk to me. It's like they know I'm a murder suspect. I don't even know how that leaked out."

Lucy glanced out the window and into the parking lot. Officer Martinez sat in an unmarked black sedan, reading a magazine. She shifted her focus back to Damien. He was as much an outsider as Max. And now with the stigma of murder attached to his name, he wouldn't get answers without her help. She straightened. It felt nice to be needed.

"And to make it worse, Max keeps asking me about my gang," Damien said. "I have no idea what the man is talking about." He pointed at the sprinkling of white in his black hair. "Doesn't he know I'm too old for a street gang?"

Lucy burst out laughing. Max was still on his Hollywood heist theory. She should explain it to Damien, but she didn't want to embarrass the police chief. Besides, she could rib Max about this supposed heist later on. "What's your next move?"

Damien grabbed hold of Lucy's shoulders and stared into her eyes. His warm brown eyes were intense, like he was trying to hypnotize her. "I have to deploy my secret weapon."

Lucy didn't like the sound of this. "What's that?"

"Lulu, you are my only hope. What have you found out?"

Lucy snorted and brushed his hands off her shoulders. What a kiss-up. "Is this off the record?"

She had no proof whatsoever about her suspects, and she didn't want her speculation splashed across the newspaper. As silly as it might sound, just having their names associated with Jason's murder could kill somebody's social standing in the community. Her mom had dealt with this plenty of times during Lucy's childhood. Small town politics were no joke.

"Off the record," Damien said. "I wouldn't want to jeopardize the investigation. It's more important to clear my name than to sell newspapers as far as I'm concerned. My uncle might believe otherwise, but he's not here."

Lucy told Damien what she'd already discussed with Stella over dinner last night.

"So our suspects are Sander, Abby, Rosalynn, and Marco," Damien said, ticking them off on his fingers. "Two couples. I wonder if a couple killed Jason together."

Lucy hadn't thought of this angle before. She had assumed the killer was working alone. "It's a possibility."

Damien pondered Lucy's words for several minutes. "What about me? Do you suspect me?"

"No," Lucy said with absolute conviction. He wasn't entirely honest with her, but he was entitled to his secrets. They hadn't known each other long enough to be an open book. Trust was built brick by brick with time.

Damien blinked like he expected a different answer. "What—"

Knock! Knock!

Lucy glanced over her shoulder. Max DeWitt and Officer Martinez filled the doorway. Her heart sank. She felt more than saw Damien straighten to his full height next to her. When the police showed up in full force, it didn't take a rocket scientist to know this was bad news.

"How can I help you, gentlemen?" Damien's voice sounded confident, but he shoved his hands into the pockets of his chinos. Were his hands trembling?

Max flicked a glance at Lucy and returned his attention to Damien. He held up a sheet of paper. "Mr. North, I have a search warrant."

14

LINE IN THE SAND

Damien staggered back a step as if Max had punched him in the gut. "What? Why?" The words came out in a croak like he could barely form the words.

"We've had an anonymous tip that said the murder weapon can be found on your premises," Max said.

Lucy reached for the search warrant. Wasn't the murder weapon the makeshift noose from the hospital sheet? This so-called tip made no sense at all. "Can I see that?"

Max jerked the paper out of her reach. "Ms. Fong, maybe you should go to your office next door." He lowered his voice, but there was a tinge of tension in it. "You don't want to get involved in this."

Lucy blew air out of her mouth audibly. If she

stayed to help Damien, Max would be annoyed with her. It might even jeopardize her friendship with the police chief, which was not good on either a personal or professional level. But if she left, Damien might not question the validity of this anonymous tip or even the legality of the search warrant. After all, a visit like this from the police was sure to rattle anyone.

"Damien, do you want me to look through the search warrant paperwork for you?" Lucy asked without taking her eyes off of Max.

The police chief stiffened imperceptibly. And Lucy wished a wormhole would open up and swallow her. She had drawn her line in the sand, and he didn't like it one bit.

Damien cleared his throat. "Ya...yes, please."

Max held out the paperwork, his expression professionally blank.

Lucy took it and scanned the contents. From the online PI class she was taking, she knew a search warrant had to specify the item and the locations the police would search. "Antifreeze?"

She glanced up and shot Max a look. He knew just as well as she did that the antifreeze only made Jason Albright sick. The EMTs got Jason to the hospital in time to pump his stomach. Did Max believe the iced tea poisoner was the same person who later killed Jason in the hospital?

Max raised an eyebrow. "You have a problem?"

Nausea rolled in the pit of Lucy's stomach. This was definitely some kind of setup, but from whom? The police or this anonymous caller? And why was Max playing along with this? Nowhere in the paperwork did it use the word "murder weapon," so Max was trying to rattle Damien. She could call the police chief out and ruin his plan, but Lucy couldn't do this to him. Straddling the line between Damien and Max was a lot more difficult than she thought it would be.

"Na...no," Lucy finally mumbled. She hoped Max had a plan, and it better not involve railroading an innocent man.

With an overwhelming sense of helplessness, Lucy watched as Max and Officer Martinez stepped around the counter and methodically combed through the newspaper office.

Damien slumped against the countertop, ignoring the police search behind him and staring out the window.

"Are you okay?" Lucy whispered. Maybe he was in shock.

"This is like a bad B-rated movie," Damien whispered back. "Any minute now, they will find something and haul me off to jail."

If the mood weren't so serious, Lucy would have

joked about the Hollywood heist. "Do you have antifreeze on your property?"

"No, but I bet the cops will find it. Someone is out to frame me, but I'm not sure who or why."

Lucy nodded in agreement. A bottle of antifreeze wasn't enough to convict Damien, but it sure could cause a lot of trouble. Someone was effectively trying to block Damien from doing his own investigation. Would this person do the same to Lucy once her interest in Jason's murder was more widely known? Was it the killer? She shivered at the thought.

"Who has been to your office lately?" she asked, pleased that her voice didn't shake.

"No one. I've closed the office since Jason Albright's death. I just opened it back up today."

Lucy thought about the break-in at the vacant property next door. A lock was not enough of a deterrent to stop a determined person from coming in.

Max approached the two of them. "Where's the printer for the newspaper? It's not in the office here."

"It's in the printing shed outside," Damien said. "Once the printers get going, the machines need ventilation. I usually keep the door and the windows open while they are running. But I only use it for last minute special editions because it's cheaper to send the paper out for printing. And half the time, they are either broken down and need maintenance or ink. The majority of my subscribers read the PDF version delivered to their inbox."

"Can you show me where it is? I need to search through there too," Max said.

Lucy had a hunch the antifreeze would be found in the shed. It didn't sound as secure as the newspaper office.

As Damien led the officers through the side door, there was a resigned look on his face. Lucy followed the men outside. The sunlight hit the metal roll-up door of the printer shed, and she squinted against the glare.

Damien opened the lock and pushed up the roll-up door. It slid up the rails, rattling and clanging. The printer shed was a single room, about ten by twenty. There were two industrial-sized printers inside, one in each corner. In the third corner were boxes of paper and ink. In the middle of the room were two long plastic tables pushed up against each other. It was probably used as a lay down area for the hot-off-the-press newspaper. Underneath the plastic table was a large wicker basket.

As the police searched the shed, Lucy's gaze swept through the room. There weren't too many places to hide the antifreeze in here. If the bottle wasn't behind one of the printers, it was probably in the wicker basket. With the setup being so painfully obvious, she wondered why Max hadn't come to the same conclusion as she did. Was he so desperate to close the case that he might be blind to everything else?

"Yah-ah," Officer Martinez yelled, jerking up from under the plastic table and bumping his head.

The wicker basket tipped onto its side, and a chicken strutted out. Its beady reddish-brown eyes stared at them without blinking. Its feathers fluffed out, making it look bigger than normal.

Lucy lowered herself onto her knees to peer under the table. "Is that Jason Albright's therapy chicken?"

Damien crouched down next to her. "It looks like it. How did it get in here?"

Lucy pointed at the door on the wall next to Damien. "Is that door locked?"

"This makes me sound like a bimbo, but I'm not sure. I don't always lock the door behind me because there's nothing valuable here. The printers are ancient machines I inherited from the previous owners. Before Jason's appearance, nothing ever happened at this end of town. We're too far from the highway for the odd random crime."

Officer Martinez reached for the chicken. It side-stepped and inched toward Lucy.

She held perfectly still. Maybe she could grab it when it came closer. Though Lucy had never raised poultry, she had plenty of experience catching and butchering a chicken for her uncle during Chinese New Year and Ching Ming, where they had to honor the ancestors with a fresh chicken.

Max paused by the side door, his gloved hand on the doorknob. His expression was openly curious with a half-smile like he expected to be entertained.

Still crouching by his corner of the table, Damien held out both hands, trying to create a human fence to keep the chicken from darting out. He sidestepped as if to give Lucy room to hold out her arms for her portion of the human fence. She ignored him and held still.

Officer Martinez crawled forward on his hands and knees, moving deeper underneath the tables. His eyes never left the chicken.

The chicken shifted its head to study both men and took a step back. It squawked a warning and backed up again, moving toward Lucy's corner of the table.

Officer Martinez launched for the chicken, reaching with both hands.

The chicken's sharp beak jerked down and landed on the fleshy part of the officer's hand between the thumb and index finger.

Officer Martinez screamed like a girly man and jerked back, bumping onto the table and lifting it several inches off the floor.

Damien flung himself at the chicken—the chicken flapped and hopped out of his reach—and belly flopped onto the concrete floor.

Lucy swooped her hands around the chicken, tucking it against her side. She stood and kept a firm grip on the animal. Just as she predicted, the chicken was docile as a baby. Jason Albright probably handled it frequently as a chick, so it was used to human touch. After all, it was a therapy chicken. She smirked at the two men getting off the floor.

Max turned to study the doorknob on the side door, but not before Lucy saw the grin on his face and the sparkle in his eyes.

Officer Martinez scooted past the wicker basket and paused to look inside. He reached in with his gloved hands and removed a plastic bottle. He scooted the rest of the way out and stood. "Boss, I found the antifreeze."

The amusement froze on Lucy's face. For a few minutes, she was caught up in the excitement of catching the chicken and forgot about why they were searching the printer shed. Her gaze flicked to Damien, who got up shakily from the ground.

"Mr. North, you'll have to come down to the station," Max said grimly, his earlier amusement long gone. "We have some questions."

As Max drove off with Damien in the patrol car, Lucy watched helplessly from the parking lot. For a smart man, Max was blind if he believed Damien would poison Jason and then leave the bottle around for the police to find it. The setup was so obvious, it bordered on the ridiculous. The killer must have accidentally let the chicken in when he stashed the bottle in the shed and didn't want to waste time chasing the animal out. Or maybe Max's hands were tied, and he had to follow protocol. Lucky for Damien, she didn't.

15

PASSING THE BUCK

Lucy glanced down at the chicken in her arm and petted its head. "Now, what am I going to do with you, My Precious? If I bring you home, Raspberry will have you for lunch. If I leave you out in the woods, another wild animal will also be after you. You're food on two legs. I guess you'll stay here until Damien gives you the boot."

She left the chicken in the printer shed and went into the PI office for a water dish. She also grabbed Stella's leftover lunch from yesterday. Once back at the printer shed, she set everything under the table by the wicker basket.

"All right, My Precious. I will see you tomorrow," Lucy said, closing the side door. She cringed at the thought of cleaning up the chicken poop, but that was Damien's problem. He should have locked his door if he didn't want animals in his printer shed.

As Lucy slid into the driver's seat of her car, her cell phone rang. She pulled out the device from her purse and accepted the call. "Stella, I'm glad you called. Max took Damien down to the station for questioning." She told her cousin about the anonymous phone call.

"Why is it always an anonymous call?" Stella said.

"Maybe the killer watched too many crime shows. I don't know if Max needs to follow protocol or if he truly believes that Damien is Jason's killer."

"We have to solve this murder pronto," Stella said.

Lucy nodded, even though her cousin couldn't see the gesture. "I agree." While she was worried about Damien, waiting at the police station would be a waste of time. He could easily get a ride back using one of the ride share apps on his phone. And until he was formally charged, he wasn't in danger yet. However, this ride down to the police station would turn him into a pariah as far as the town folks were concerned.

She mentally ran through the list of suspects again. "I'm meeting Calla and Abby at the Chinese Temple for a tour. Why don't you come along and distract Calla? I want to talk to Abby alone."

"Okey-dokey. I'm getting quite good at distracting people." There was a hint of pride in Stella's voice.

"Please don't set off the fire alarm at the temple. It's a historic building, and we can't afford to pay for damages. You're lucky the Fisherman's Catch didn't press charges."

"They have no evidence. Anyone could have thrown the burning cigarette into the trash bin. I wasn't the only one in the women's restroom."

Lucy ground her teeth. There was no point in arguing. "I'm leaving now. I'll pick you up in a few minutes."

During the ten-minute drive to the edge of town, Lucy and Stella hashed and rehashed what they already knew about the murder investigation.

"We are getting nowhere in this conversation," Lucy said. "I can call Rosalynn and invite her to coffee, but how do we get in touch with Marco?"

"I know where his mother lives. Doesn't he live with her?" Stella asked.

"Do you know her?"

"We're not friends, but we always chatted when she came by for her monthly prescription at the pharmacy."

"Then why didn't you say so earlier? This could have prevented you from starting the fire at the restaurant."

"First, there was no fire. Just a lot of smoke.

Second, you didn't ask if I knew the Domenico family."

Lucy rubbed her temple and winced at the pounding headache. She took a deep breath and let it out slowly, praying for patience. "Do you know Marco?"

"No, I just know his mother. When you're questioning her, you'll have to be careful. I think her brother is in the mob."

Lucy pulled into the gravel parking lot for the Chinese Temple. She turned to Stella and said, "Her brother is a senior citizen. What can he do to me?"

"He might still have contacts in the mob, and someone younger can take us out," Stella said, unbuckling her seatbelt and opening the car door.

Lucy slammed the door shut. "You're right. It's stupid for me to underestimate someone because of their age."

They followed a dirt path through the grove of trees until it opened out into a wildflower meadow. The flimsy wood building in the middle of it looked more like a miner shack than a temple.

"It's...uh, rustic," Stella finally said. "I was expecting a tiered pagoda."

"Me too, which doesn't make any sense," Lucy said. "The Chinese settled here during the gold rush and later worked on the railroad. They wouldn't have the resources or support to build a foreign structure like a pagoda. And they probably built the temple to look like this so it could blend in with the other buildings at the time."

"It's on a piece of prime real estate though," Stella said, taking a deep breath. "You can smell the Pacific Ocean from here. I bet if you keep walking, you'll end up on the edge of a cliff and see the ocean."

Up close, the shack was bigger than it appeared, probably the size of a small banquet hall. It could easily hold fifty or sixty people. Beyond the shack were multiple smaller brick buildings, connected by overhead breezeways and courtyards. Calla Louie was curled up on a rocking chair on the shady part of the porch in front of the shack. She hopped out of the chair like a piston with a hand out for a handshake.

Lucy felt like a decrepit old lady lumbering up the steps to the porch. There was no way she could move like Calla, no matter how many Jane Fonda exercise videos she did. She introduced Stella.

The two women shook hands. Next to Stella with her Faye height, Calla looked like a child with her chin-length black hair and straight bangs.

Calla cocked her head, studying Lucy and Stella. "Is the haircut a job requirement? Like a uniform?"

Lucy touched her pixie cut with its red streaks. These days, she always felt like she showed up to the prom wearing the same dress as the prom queen. But what else could she do? It would hurt her cousin's feelings if Lucy changed her hairstyle.

Stella patted her hair and preened. "Isn't it cute? We're twins."

Lucy turned away from the discussion to study the double front doors. She didn't want to inadvertently say something mean. On top of the doorway and on either side hung red-painted wood boards with Chinese calligraphy in gold lettering—probably blessings of a sort.

To the left were rows and rows of little brass plates on the wall next to the front door. Lucy took a step closer and scanned the writing. There were names of couples, family trusts, and even some nonprofit organizations. They looked like a list of donors for the Chinese Temple. Her gaze went past a plate and immediately jerked back. Marco Domenico?

"These are the names of our donors," Calla said. "We are trying to restore the temple. After decades of incense and candle smoke, there is a layer of soot on everything. It takes money to restore things properly, especially the fragile gold leafing and the mother-of-pearl inlays."

Lucy pointed at the plate. "Is this Marco Domenico, the IT guy?"

Calla nodded. "I was engaged to him when we

did the restoration for this part of the temple. He probably felt obligated to make a donation. So his name is on the wall of donors."

"Why did you break up?" Stella asked.

Calla gave her a sideways glance. "Not to be rude, but it's really none of your business."

Stella blushed and averted her gaze. Though she was an extrovert who liked to talk just to talk, she had spent most of her life behind the pharmacy counter and cared for her aging parents. She could be socially awkward at times. Maybe this was why she was hesitant to take up the mantle for the family business.

Lucy's skin was much thicker. It would take more than a stony stare and a few harsh words for her to give up on a possible lead. She softened her tone, hoping it sounded inviting. "Sorry, Stella is just concerned. A good friend of ours is dating him. Something about the guy doesn't feel right, but I just can't put my finger on what's wrong with him."

From behind Calla, Stella gave Lucy a thumbs-up sign. She drifted to the other end of the porch to examine the wildflowers growing on the lawn. Even though she was pretending to snap photos, Lucy knew Stella had no interest in gardens or plants. She was probably eavesdropping on the conversation.

Calla shrugged. She didn't appear to be in a

gossipy mood. Or maybe she wasn't one of those types who kiss and tell.

"Is it because he is still living with his mother?" Lucy mused aloud, hoping to continue the conversation.

Silence.

Lucy waited with a concerned expression on her face. Sometimes people would fill the silence with chatter without being aware of it.

After a long pause, Calla said, "I didn't have a problem with Marco living at home. It's common in Asian families for adult children to live with their parents to save money for a down payment on a house."

Lucy nodded. "I moved back to my uncle's after college. He had a place in San Francisco China-town." She didn't add that she had her own apart-ment unit in the building and never paid rent. Her uncle had taken care of Lucy better than either one of her parents ever did.

Calla's eyes brightened. "Then you know what I mean."

Lucy nodded again. She wasn't sure what Calla meant, but Lucy must have passed some kind of test. By mentioning her Chinese uncle, did she appear less like a stranger? Or was it living in Chinatown? Sometimes she still didn't understand the intricacies of the Chinese community.

"My problem is with Marco being under his mother's thumb," Calla said. "I didn't see this disappearing after our marriage. As a matter of fact, I wasn't even sure he would be willing to move out. And I certainly was not moving in."

Lucy whistled under her breath. Holy Toledo! This was worse than she imagined. Surely, Rosalynn had figured this out by now. Was she planning to move in with her mother-in-law? "Tiger mom?"

"The opposite. When Marco was young, he was sickly. Later he became an only child when his older brother drowned in an accident," Calla said. "I guess the two of them got into the habit of his mother helicoptering around him. In some ways, I don't think they ever got over the older brother's death."

"What about his father?"

"I have no idea. Marco never mentioned his father. Maybe he walked out on them."

Lucy opened her mouth, but—

"Looks like we're all here," Abby called out from behind Lucy. Footsteps approached the porch.

Lucy glanced over her shoulder. Fabulous. The mayor's wife apparently had perfect timing. Maybe this was why everyone said she was Sander's shadow.

Calla's face became neutrally blank. "Let's start the tour." While her tone was still melodious, it became brisk and no-nonsense. She wasn't here for small talk.

The four of them stepped into the Chinese Temple.

"This is the main worship room," Calla said, gesturing to the stoneware figurines of deities in an altar on the wall in front of them.

Of the five deities, Lucy only recognized Buddha by his jolly belly. Like the Egyptians and Greeks, traditional Chinese worshiped a pantheon of gods and goddesses, including the humans who became gods for their grand achievements. She would need a cheat sheet to keep them all straight in her mind.

In front of the figurines was a long narrow rosewood table with candlestick holders for the ceremonial red candles and an incense pot with burnt joss sticks in it. There were red banners with gold calligraphy on the walls, probably blessings. Lucy didn't recognize any of the characters, but her Chinese was limited to picking out dishes on a restaurant menu. And soot covered everything.

"You're pagans?" Abby said. She didn't bother hiding the incredulity in her voice.

Stella mouthed behind their backs, "Catfight." Her eyes twinkled like she already had a popcorn bucket in front of her.

Lucy sighed. Her day was bad enough already. She didn't need it to be worse. "We're here to discuss the ownership of the Monkey King artifact. Anything else is irrelevant."

Calla's nose flared like she had inhaled the aroma of a dead fish. "Let's get on with this."

Abby raised an eyebrow at the altar. "Where exactly are you planning to place this priceless treasure?"

Lucy glanced around the room. There was nothing worth stealing, so the only security measure was the locks on the front and side doors.

Calla pointed to a spot underneath a red banner on the left wall. "I can have someone build a little platform for it."

Lucy gave Calla a sideways glance. Was she joking? No, Calla appeared perfectly serious.

Abby burst out laughing. Stella's eyes looked like they were about to fall out of their sockets.

"Um, the Monkey King artifact is worth a quarter-million dollars," Lucy said.

Calla stared at Lucy blankly.

"Anyone could walk off with it," Abby said. "You can't expect the town to turn over something this valuable when there's no security here."

Calla bristled at the tone. "Your people have already stolen—"

"Whoa! Let's not go there." Lucy held up the universal timeout sign with her hands. "Whatever happened before was before our time here on earth. We're not going back in time."

"We're here to discuss the best location for displaying the artifact," Stella said. "And given the lack of security, the temple might not be the best place for it."

"But the artifact belongs with my people," Calla said.

"The artifact was found on town property," Abby said. "The Chinese community has no claim on it."

Both women spun around and looked at Lucy, waiting for her comment.

This discussion was beyond Lucy's pay grade. Like a chump, she wasn't even getting paid for this headache. "None of us here has the background to establish the ownership of the artifact. The lawyers would have to hash out the ownership of the artifact."

"I thought you were on our side," Calla said.

Lucy held up both hands, palms out. "You can't claim ownership just because the Monkey King is a Chinese deity. The character is an amalgam of Indian and Chinese cultures. It started when merchants brought the Buddhist sutras to China. You don't see the Indian community claiming ownership of this artifact."

Abby crossed her arms, a pleased expression on her face. "Exactly. We're looking for a place to display the artifact to the public. Putting it here in the temple would hide it."

Calla glared at Lucy. "I don't need you to lecture me on the history of the Monkey King."

"I have seen enough," Abby said. "I'll report my findings to Sander." She spun on her heels and marched toward the front doors.

"I'm sorry," Lucy said. "I don't have any influence on what the town does with the artifact."

Lucy dashed out the door, hoping to catch Abby before she got to her car. She heard Stella making her apologies behind her. The entire visit was ghastly. It had resolved nothing, and now the town might have a lawsuit on their hands. She didn't know why Sander thought his wife could represent the town. He should have been here, doing his job. Lucy was coming to the conclusion that not only did Sander look like Santa Claus, but he also preferred to tinker in his office rather than deal with the hard stuff.

16

KISSING GAME

"Wait!" Lucy called out, jogging up to the mayor's wife.

Abby kept up her brisk walk on the dirt path back to the parking lot. "They have a canceled appointment at the beauty salon. I have to get going if I want to make it. This time of year, everyone is getting their hair done before the Christmas dinners and parties."

Lucy had forgotten that the holidays were around the corner. The signs were there with all the decorations around town, but it didn't register in her conscious mind. She had spent the last two Christmases alone in her apartment. It was too much to be around her foster family and their warmth with her uncle in the hospital. And when he died, everything became dark like she was at the bottom of a deep well.

She blinked. The dark times were done. No point in thinking about it now. She made a mental note to start gift shopping and forced her attention back to the investigation. "Someone hired an assassin to kill Jason on the dark web."

Abby frowned. "What is the dark web? Is that when your computer goes into night mode and your browser turns dark?" She appeared genuinely confused.

Lucy ignored Abby's questions. "Several thousand dollars changed hands. The FBI is taking this very seriously."

Abby paused mid-step. "Why are you telling me this?" She glanced at her watch. "I really have to go. If I miss my appointment, I can't get in for another two weeks. We can chat next time."

"Lulu!" Stella called out from behind. "Don't leave without me."

Lucy glanced over her shoulder. "I know. I'll meet you at the car."

When Lucy spun back to talk to Abby, the mayor's wife was already at the edge of the parking lot. Lucy slowed to a stop and bent over to catch her breath. How in the world did Abby have the stamina to move this fast? She was at least ten years older than Lucy.

Stella glided over on her long legs. "Did you talk to her?" She wasn't even breathless.

Lucy shook her head. "She has an appointment at the beauty salon."

Stella nodded. "So that's why she's rushing out of here. Makes sense. I can't get an appointment until after Christmas." She brushed her hair back into place. "I guess I'll have to keep this haircut a little longer. Hey, we can get matching ugly Christmas sweaters. Wouldn't that be cute?"

Lucy stretched her lips into what she hoped was a grin. No, it didn't sound cute. "Sounds like fun."

"All right. You leave the shopping to me. I'll pick out something really nice for us."

Lucy gave Stella a thumbs up sign. She really had no words for the horrible idea, but she didn't want to disappoint her cousin. "Do you think Sander is still in his office?"

Stella shook her head. "It's Friday afternoon. No one puts in a full day at City Hall. That's how government employees work, you know."

"Where can we find him?"

"His home? When he is not working, he's a bit of a homebody."

"It's worth a try. I want to talk to Sander without Abby hovering."

Stella rubbed her stomach. "Don't you think we should have lunch first? I'm starving."

Lucy checked the time. It was already one thirty. She dug out a granola bar and tossed it to Stella. We've got to strike while the iron is hot, or in this case, while the cat is away. We might not get another chance to talk to Sander alone."

They got into the car, and Lucy followed Stella's directions to the Frasiers' home. It was a colonial with white cedar shingles weathered to a light gray and blue shutters at all the windows. The house stood at the end of a long driveway, its front hidden in the shadow by the foliage of three ancient sycamore trees. A decked-out truck was parked in the driveway.

Lucy drove past the house slowly.

"You missed the house," Stella said, pointing to the colonial.

"I know." Lucy parked half a block away on the side of the road. "It's time we get into stealth mode. A surprise visit might turn up something."

Stella frowned. "You're probably right, Archie. It looks like Sander has company. That's not his truck in the driveway."

Lucy raised an eyebrow. "Maybe he invited his girlfriend over while his wife was out of the house."

"I don't believe it. Ever since Sander married Abby, he hasn't even looked at another woman."

Lucy left her car doors unlocked in case they needed a hasty getaway. In this part of town, the folks were more worried that Lucy might steal their car instead of the other way around. "We'll just have to see. Lead us to his living room windows, Nero."

Stella beamed. She thought of herself as the great detective and Lucy as her sidekick. "If we're caught, it would be very embarrassing. I wouldn't know how to explain it to my old friend. But we're private investigators and sneaking around is part of the job. Maybe I can pretend I'm going senile."

Lucy chuckled. "Can we say we got the wrong house?"

Stella gave Lucy a deadpan stare. "And there goes the reputation of Faye Investigations. Down the toilet. Well, that is not happening on my watch."

While they strolled up to the house, Lucy scanned the neighborhood. Many respectable founding families lived in this part of town where the homes were on large lots and passed down from one generation to the next. Since the Fayes weren't quite respectable back in those days, they couldn't even come within spitting distance of this area.

No one was on the street, and the other homes were tucked safely behind their foliage of trees and shrubs. A person could commit a crime in broad daylight, and no one would be the wiser. Lucy didn't know if living in such a neighborhood was a blessing or a curse.

They were about to walk up the driveway when

the front door opened. Lucy jumped behind the sycamore, hoping the tree trunk would hide her wide derrière. Stella dropped low onto the ground like she was about to do an army crawl over the tree roots. Lucy held her breath, waiting for Sander to call out to them.

Muffled music floated out from the house. After several heartbeats, Lucy exhaled through her mouth. That was close. She glanced down at Stella, who was lifting her head to peek around the tree roots. Lucy moved her head slightly to the left and peered around the thick trunk.

Sander and a man stood next to the decked-out pickup truck on the driveway. The car door was opened, and the man looked as if he was about to get in but was reluctant to leave.

"That's the deputy mayor," Stella whispered from the ground. "What is he doing here?"

Lucy studied the two men. There was something strange about their body language, but she couldn't quite put her finger on it. The two men laughed at a joke, and Sander patted the deputy mayor on the shoulder. They had obviously worked together for many years and developed a close friendship. Most men she knew didn't get inside each other's physical space unless they played a contact sport.

The deputy mayor got into the truck and slammed the door shut. He started the engine, rolled the window down, and leaned out. Sander reached in and pulled the deputy mayor's head close for a long kiss.

Lucy's jaw dropped. Sander was gay? Having lived in San Francisco for more than half her life, Lucy had plenty of gay friends. But they were openly gay, unlike the mayor. Sander still portrayed himself as a family man with a wife and a grown child. He was expecting his first grand-child. His career was based on this wholesome family image. Was this what Jason had over the mayor? And did Abby know about her husband's inclination?

The pickup truck backed out of the driveway and was gone in less than a heartbeat, leaving Sander at the top of the suspect list.

Stella got up from the ground and waved a hand overhead. "Yoo-hoo!"

Sander glanced over at the sycamore tree and turned ashen.

Stella loped over to join the mayor in the drive-way. Lucy trotted to keep up with her cousin's longer legs.

Up close, Lucy saw sweat dotting Sander's fore-head and upper lip. He looked like he just ate a rotten egg.

"Is this why you wanted to kill Jason Albright?" Stella said. "He knows your dirty little secret."

Lucy groaned inwardly. Her cousin's lack of social grace would get them in trouble someday.

Sander sputtered, turning even paler. "It's not what you think."

"Then explain it to us," Lucy whispered, hoping she sounded reasonable. She was curious to see how the mayor, a lifelong politician, would spin the story. "How did Jason find out you are gay?"

Silence.

Stella opened her mouth, but Lucy gave her a pointed look. Her cousin reluctantly closed her mouth and waited.

Sander's shoulders dropped, and he sighed audibly. "I go camping every year at a remote site in Nevada with other men like me. In all the decades I have gone, I've never seen anyone from our town." He licked his lower lip as if trying to buy some time. "Last year, I ran into Jason at the gas station outside of the campground. He must have put two and two together because he started blackmailing me when I got home."

Lucy frowned. "From a brief encounter at the gas station, Jason figured out you're gay? How is that possible?"

"Maybe the town folks talk." Sander shrugged. "The nearest town is twenty minutes away from the campground, but we have had this annual trip for the last twenty years. First, it started with me and a few buddies, and now it has morphed into a hundred of us."

"Does Abby know?" Stella asked.

Sander nodded. "I told her in high school."

"And the two of you got married anyway?" Stella asked with incredulity in her voice.

"Abby wanted a father for the baby, and she wanted to leave her parents' home. I have been a good husband and father." Sander rubbed a hand over his face. "When Jason started blackmailing me, I thought about telling him to go ahead with his threats, but Abby stopped me. She doesn't want the truth to come out."

"What did you do next?" Lucy whispered. Sander seemed to be in a trance like he was off-loading a burden he had carried far too long. "Did you try to hire an assassin to kill him?"

Sander's lips twisted into a bitter smile. "It was a middle of the night Jerry Maguire moment. I regretted it the next morning, so you can imagine my relief when I found out it was a scam. The assassin"—he made air quotes with his fingers—"has a video of me watching porn. If I don't give him more money, he will send the video to all the people in my phone's Contacts. Apparently, I got mixed up in two Internet scams. Let me tell you, this was a very expensive lesson to learn."

Stella snickered behind her hands.

Lucy shot her a warning glance and returned her attention to Sander. "The FBI warned Jason about the assassination contract. I don't think it is quite over yet, especially now that Jason died."

Sander grimaced. "His death has nothing to do with me. I found out from my IT guy that my money went to an offshore account in Russia."

"Who is your IT guy?" Stella asked.

"Marco Domenico. He said I got scammed, and no attempt was made," Sander said.

Lucy raised an eyebrow. "Are you sure about that? Someone spiked Jason's tea with antifreeze. That's how he ended up in the hospital in the first place."

Sander shook his head. "That wasn't me. And the assassin board is not a real place to hire someone. Once I realized my mistake, I deleted the post and closed my account. Nothing happened."

"While that might be true, you do have a strong motive to kill him," Lucy said.

"I don't care who knows anymore," Sander said. "My parents are dead. My son is grown. And I don't need to be the mayor. I never needed the job. It was other people's expectations that got me here. And if Abby wants a divorce, she can have one. I don't care enough to kill someone to keep this a secret."

"Then how do you explain hiring an assassin?" Stella asked.

"I've already explained it," Sander said. "It was a middle of the night mistake. That's why they run infomercials in the middle of the night, trying to get insomniacs to buy things. And that's what happened to me. Luckily, I got scammed. If anything had happened to Jason on my account, I would have been horrified."

"How did Jason get a town job?" Lucy asked. "We thought he blackmailed you into hiring him."

Sander frowned. "He worked for the town? What position?"

"He was your new maintenance worker," Stella said.

"I don't know about the hiring," Sander said. "It's too many levels below me."

As Sander went back inside his home, Lucy mentally checked him off the suspect list. She believed him. The times had changed enough that even close-minded small-town folks were aware of the LGBT community. And for someone like Sander, if things got bad enough, he could afford to pick up and move to a place that would embrace him. Jason was not a big enough threat to Sander.

17

AN AMATEUR

After breakfast at the Shoreline Café with Stella the next morning, Lucy drove to the PI office to put out food and water for the chicken in the printer shed. The rooster popped his head out of the wicker basket but didn't get out to greet her. Not even a quick chirp. Some therapy chicken. It was starting to act like the Little Emperor at home.

Lucy ran back to her car and drove them to the Domenico home. The GPS unit on the dashboard guided them to the other side of the mountain to a newer subdivision with tiny lots. The residents had an ocean view and had to drive thirty minutes or more to access the beach. This would have been prime real estate in San Francisco but was considered a cheaper area by the local residents. The house was a modern ranch house situated in the middle of the subdivision. It looked almost like every other home on the street, except for the patch of dried motor oil on its driveway.

When Stella rang the doorbell, Mrs. Domenico swung the door wide open and exclaimed in delight. "My dear, Estelle," Mrs. Domenico said, enveloping Stella into a bear hug. "Long time no see. Come in, come in."

Mrs. Domenico was in her early seventies. She was short and stout, barely reaching Stella's armpit. Her silver hair was tied up in a loose bun on the back of her head. In it, she had woven a red ribbon and black feathers. It was cool looking but wholly unexpected. Her warm brown eyes were fierce. She looked as if she could whip out a rolling pin and bash someone on the head with it. She noticed Lucy for the first time and gestured at her. "And this, your daughter?"

Lucy suppressed a smirk. This was a blow to her cousin's ego. Stella liked to think of herself as an older sister.

"Lucy is my cousin's daughter, but she's more like a younger sister to me," Stella said. "We're close in age."

Mrs. Domenico's expression didn't change, but

her eyes twinkled with amusement. "Come. Marco is bringing over Rosie for dinner later, so I made cannolis for her."

As Lucy stepped through the living room and into the kitchen, the scent of vanilla and deep-fried pastry dough hit her nose. She sniffed appreciatively, and her mouth began to water. It was the weekend. She was entitled to one cheat day. Would it be considered unprofessional to accept dessert from a suspect's mother?

When Marco came into the kitchen from the connecting garage door a few minutes later, Lucy sat at the kitchen table, stuffing her face with a cannoli. Stella had declined the treat.

Mrs. Domenico got up and exclaimed over the bouquet of flowers and bags of produce from the farmer's market. "What a good boy you are, Marco."

"Ma, you didn't tell me you were expecting company," Marco said. He didn't quite scowl, but his expression wasn't friendly.

Lucy didn't know what to make of it. She gave him a tiny wave. "Hi, Marco. Remember me? I am Rosalynn's friend."

"What are you doing here?" Marco said cautiously. He placed the bags on the kitchen island and started unloading them.

Lucy lifted her plate. "Eating cannoli. I didn't

realize my cousin Stella and your mom were friends."

Marco turned to his mother. "Ma, I have to talk to Lucy for a few minutes. You think you can put this away by yourself?"

Mrs. Domenico flapped her hands dismissively. "Go, go. I'll take care of it."

Marco tilted his head toward the connecting garage door. "Let me show you the yard."

Lucy picked up the half-eaten cannoli and followed him outside. No way was she leaving this goodie behind. It tasted even better than the cannolis she got at the Italian bakery a few blocks from her apartment in San Francisco.

Marco led them to the sapling in the middle of the lawn. He bent down to fiddle with the sprinkler head. "Rosie told me you're a private investigator. Did she hire you to check up on me?"

Lucy swallowed the bite in her mouth. Where did this come from? "Why would Rosalynn need to investigate you? Do you have anything to hide?"

Marco straightened and narrowed his eyes. "If she isn't investigating me, then you must be working for her ex. Since he is dead, why are you still poking your nose in my business?"

Lucy didn't know what to say. The guy was a paranoid loon. "I'm not interested in your business." This was a bald-faced lie, but she didn't want to antagonize him. "I came back to town because my mom is in the hospital. And my family has been private investigators for generations. It's not a secret. If it makes you feel any better, I'm not actually a private investigator. I am an internet marketing consultant. All my gigs in town are related to marketing and e-commerce for the local businesses."

Marco took a deep breath and seemed to relax visibly. "Sorry, I know I sounded crazy, but this relationship with Rosie is important to me. I'm planning to pop the question this evening, and I don't want anything to mess things up."

Lucy raised an eyebrow. For a brief moment, she wondered if Rosalynn liked being called Rosie or was this nickname forced upon her. "If it were me, I wouldn't want a proposal in front of my future mother-in-law."

"No, of course not. I'm not that dense. After dinner, I was planning to take Rosie out for ice cream at the pier."

"That sounds romantic." Not as romantic as dinner for two at the Sea King restaurant and then a walk along the beach. What kind of man asked his mother to cook and sit down at the proposal dinner? "I guess it's a good thing Jason can no longer interfere with your relationship."

Marco's hands curled into fists. The guy's mood

was worse than a swinging pendulum. "So, you are investigating Jason's death. I have nothing to say to you. If you don't leave Rosie or me alone, you'll be sorry."

Lucy's body temperature shot up, and a bead of sweat rolled down her back. Maybe there was some truth that the Domenico family had a mob connection. Lucy was already in over her head, so she might as well take the full tumble. He probably wouldn't strangle her on his front lawn with his mother and Stella in the kitchen. Lucy glanced up and down the street. They were alone. The muscles in her legs tensed, waiting for flight. "Did you have lunch with Jason at the hospital cafeteria last week?"

Marco snorted. "You are right. You're not a private investigator. If you were, you would know that I was out of town last week at a network security training in LA. Do you want to see my hotel receipt?"

Lucy blinked. He had an alibi? A hotel stay was easy enough to verify, but it would require a drive down to LA and money to loosen up an underpaid employee's lips.

"Well, do you want to see the receipt?" Marco asked.

Lucy shook her head. Since Marco had a hotel receipt, he probably was out of town. "No. I never suspected you." Did she sound convincing? "There's a rumor that Jason had lunch with someone in the cafeteria before his death. I thought maybe the two of you had a man-to-man talk and came to an understanding. Rosalynn really cares about you, and I don't want this rumor to ruin things for the two of you."

Marco appeared mollified. "I'm glad we had this chat, Lucy. Seeing as you're one of Rosie's oldest friends, we're bound to spend time together in the future. And I don't want things to be weird between us."

Lucy smiled, hoping she appeared relaxed. Weird was an understatement. She hoped they never spent any time together in a social situation. It was too bad Marco was no longer a suspect.

As Marco strolled back to the kitchen, Lucy went through her suspect list. With Sander and Marco off the list, this left only Abby or Rosalynn. Lucy couldn't imagine Abby having lunch with Jason at the hospital cafeteria. As the mayor's wife, folks would recognize her and talk about her date with a younger man. If Abby had to meet with Jason, it would be at a secluded location away from prying eyes.

Even though the Albrights were separated, folks would think nothing of Rosalynn having lunch with Jason. It was not even worth gossiping about. Did

Rosalynn poison Jason's iced tea? And did she strangle him with the hospital sheet later when her first attempt failed?

Lucy found it surprising that Marco didn't appear to suspect Rosalynn of killing Jason. If she did turn out to be the murderer, how would he react? And would he blame Lucy for shining a light at the cafeteria lunch date?

AFTER SHE DROPPED STELLA OFF, Lucy went home to catch up on housework. Her mom had a mild case of OCD, and Lucy didn't want Mom to come home to a dirty house on the off chance she woke up from her coma. While the laundry dried, she went back to the kitchen and called Damien. It immediately went to voicemail. She left a message and then texted him. Would she appear a little too desperate if she showed up at his house?

After all, it had only been twenty-four hours, and the two of them weren't exactly a couple. For some reason, Lucy had expected Damien to check in with her when he finished his business at the police station. Something as simple as a quick text to ease her mind. Maybe she expected too much.

Or maybe Damien was still held up at the police

station. Surely Max hadn't charged Damien for murder based on a flimsy setup? The printer shed was as secure as a revolving door. Anyone could have put the bottle of antifreeze in there. And to make it even more confusing, the antifreeze poisoning was an attempted murder weapon.

Raspberry nudged Lucy and dropped a dead meadow mouse by her foot. He sat back on his haunches, a proud hunter providing for his family.

Lucy sneezed. When was the last time she took her allergy medicine? And why was the Little Emperor trying to butter her up? "Good job, big boy." She reached out to pet him, but he turned in a flash and stalked out of the room with his tail up, leaving her hand hanging midair. Fabulous. She just got played. The cat had to be bipolar.

She got up and grabbed some paper towels to clean up the gift. After she scrubbed her hands twice with soap, she grabbed her cell phone and texted Max.

Can I buy you dinner?

Max texted back.

I would love to, but I have a press conference in a few minutes.

Lucy frowned at the message. Maybe this was why Damien didn't return her call. He was probably at this press conference too. But their small town didn't generate the kind of crime that would need a press conference, unless... Her fingers tapped out a message.

DID YOU MAKE AN ARREST FOR JASON'S MURDER?

Max replied.

NO COMMENT.

Lucy rolled her eyes even though Max couldn't see her. If she worked at it, she was pretty sure she could get a comment.

HOW ABOUT A LATE DINNER AFTERWARD?

There was no reply for a long moment. Finally Max texted back a reply.

OKAY, BUT I HAVE A FEELING YOU'RE NOT GOING TO WANT TO EAT WITH ME LATER.

And with that cryptic message, Lucy's heart sank. She didn't know how she knew, but she knew. The police had arrested Damien.

Lucy began pacing in the kitchen. Now what? She had no doubt in her mind that Max got the wrong person, and he knew he got the wrong person. What was the endgame here?

Or maybe this had nothing to do with the crime. Max was still on his one-year probation as their newly minted police chief. He was the embodiment of a Boy Scout troop leader. He genuinely wanted to do good, but was she giving him too much credit?

She had to do something. There was the possibility that she might get in the way of a police sting, but she couldn't live with herself if Max didn't investigate this case properly.

Lucy called Rosalynn. There was a high possibility that her childhood friend had lunch with Jason and poisoned his iced tea. He wouldn't have accepted a drink from anyone else.

When Rosalynn picked up the phone, Lucy forced a cheerful smile on her face. "Hey, girl. Want to have dinner together tonight?"

"I'm sorry. I'm having dinner with Marco and his mother," Rosalynn said.

Lucy winced inwardly. She had forgotten about the ghastly proposal dinner. They made plans to meet for coffee the next morning at the Shoreline Bakery. Lucy didn't look forward to hearing all the boring details of the proposal, but it might make Rosalynn let down her guard.

Knock! Knock!

Stella's face appeared in the window of the back door. She must have walked over, or she would have come in through the front.

Lucy got up and opened the door.

"Max arrested Damien," they said in unison together.

Stella smiled. "I told you we're like twins. We're even starting to think alike."

Lucy didn't want to get into this discussion again. "I don't understand how arresting Damien would help capture the real murderer."

"With Damien behind bars, the killer might feel safe and slip up," Stella said.

Lucy considered Stella's words. If Damien had truly been arrested, his rich eccentric uncle would kick up a fuss. Even if the uncle couldn't get into town, he would undoubtedly unleash a lawyer in a bespoke suit to deal with it.

So this meant the two men were working together, and Damien was consenting to the arrest. Would Damien really be in a jail cell, or would he quietly slip out to investigate on the sly? And would he contact Lucy?

But the two men clearly hadn't thought through this harebrained scheme. Damien had no motive for killing Jason in the first place. The two men had never interacted publicly. And if the motive released at the press conference was the Hollywood heist theory, the killer would be stupid to believe it. Max would have to play the bumbling small-town cop to the hilt to make this one fly. If they had to rely on his amateur acting skills, they were in trouble.

18

BIG NUGGETS

During the drive to the historic downtown area, Stella checked the online newspaper forum. There was already chatter about the press conference.

"BigNugget5 thinks Damien is guilty because he smiles," Stella said. "I have a feeling BigNugget5 is threatened by Damien. Maybe he's got itty-bitty nuggets."

Lucy chuckled. There were moments when Stella sounded just like her foster grandma.

The historic downtown area hadn't changed much since Lucy's childhood, but the strip of shoreline a quarter-mile to the west had developed into a tourist destination with access to the beach and the marina. The dozen bed and breakfast Victorian homes proudly displayed Christmas trees in their windows and wreaths on the front doors.

The police station was once a small three-bedroom house situated between City Hall and the Shoreline bakery. The city bought the building more than twenty years ago when it went up for auction. When the police department expanded to its current staff of three and filled the assigned two rooms in the basement of City Hall, they were relocated to the small house.

Lucy parked in the public lot behind the station, and they walked around to the front. On the lawn of the police station was a podium with five metal chairs facing it. Lucy wasn't sure who was expected to show up. The only newspaper reporter was in a jail cell. And she doubted that out-of-town reporters were interested in this homicide. Not when murders were as common as pigeons in a big city. Who was this show set up for?

A woman with flaming dyed red hair and long red fingernails came out of the police station. She appeared to be in her early twenties and probably graduated from high school the same year as Lucy's younger sister. She began to fold up one of the chairs.

"Hi, April," Lucy said, approaching the clerk.

The younger woman cocked a hip and placed a hand on it. "Yes? Can I help you?" The words sounded polite, but the tone implied that Lucy better not ask for something difficult.

"We're here for the press conference. Where is Max?" Lucy asked.

"We were done five minutes ago." April turned her back to Lucy and began to drag the chair up the front steps.

"Is Max inside?" Lucy asked.

"I don't know where the boss went," April said over her shoulder. "I'm not his keeper."

Lucy turned to Stella. "I'm going inside to look for Max. Why don't you go to the bakery and pick up some gossip?" She didn't think Max would be comfortable discussing the murder investigation in front of her cousin.

Stella gave a salute. "Sure thing, Archie."

As Lucy strolled in, she noticed that the Christmas wreath hung in the center of the glass inserts at the front door matched the Christmas tree next to the fireplace inside. The living room was about eighteen feet by eighteen feet, one of those open floor plans that combined multiple rooms into a great room. The police department converted the space into a place of business by strategic furniture placement.

A short wood bench ran along one wall of the foyer with the bulletin board on the opposite wall for posting community events and mugshots of people wanted for local crimes. A counter faced the front door, barring polite folks from wandering in but still retaining an open and inviting environment. The sugary sweet aroma from the bakery next door drifted in through the windows, which were cracked open to let in the fresh air. Behind the counter were three empty desks. April probably took the chair to a storage room.

Lucy went around the counter and made her way down the hall, past the first bedroom, which was converted into two holding cells with iron bars, bolted cots, and wall-mounted sinks and toilets. They were empty. Where was Damien?

A noise came from the second bedroom door, the door opened, and Max stepped out, holding equipment for a wire.

Max blinked. "Why did April let you come back here?"

"She didn't. She's busy putting away the chairs, and I snuck in here," Lucy said, not wanting to get the clerk in trouble. "What is going on here? We both know the real murder weapon wasn't the antifreeze."

"Shhh!" Max said, glancing over Lucy's shoulder, probably to check to make sure no one was around. He turned and headed toward the master bedroom that got converted to a conference room.

"We both know Damien isn't guilty. Why did you arrest him?" Lucy said, dogging Max's steps.

"Are you sure about that?" Max said over his shoulder. "Mr. North confessed to the crime."

"The two of you are scheming something together," Lucy said.

Max opened the conference room door. There was a long table and several chairs inside. "Did you hear that, North?"

Damien sat at the conference table, playing with a paperclip. He straightened when he saw Lucy. "Lulu! It's about time you joined us. What took you so long?" Damien said. He pulled out the chair next to him and patted the seat. "You're just in time for our powwow."

Lucy's gaze swiveled between the two men. Were they serious? She studied their faces again. Yep, they were. She sank down onto the chair next to Damien. "The two of you have been working together all this time?" She felt like a chump for worrying about Damien. "There was no anonymous tip, right?"

Damien looked embarrassed. "I wanted to tell you, Lulu. But Max is in charge."

Lucy glared at Max. "I thought we were friends."

"We are friends," Max said. "But I have a job to do. And I can't let friends keep me from doing it."

Lucy crossed her arms and harrumphed. She was angry at herself for wasting her energy on these men. "All right. I'll bite. What is all this about? Or is it still need to know?"

Damien leaned in. "We're going to get Rosalynn Albright to confess to murdering her husband."

Lucy raised an eyebrow. "Is that right?"

Max ticked off the points on his fingers. "She has a new man. He is planning to propose tonight. And she will get close to a half-million dollars from Jason's life insurance policy. Plus, she had lunch with Jason Albright at the hospital cafeteria. One of the workers saw them together. She's our killer."

"How did you know about the proposal?" Lucy asked. "I just found out about it this morning."

"Mrs. Domenico told everyone at the fish market yesterday," Damien said.

"She also mentioned the life insurance policy," Max said.

Lucy's eyes widened. Was this why Marco wanted to get married now? For the money? She felt bad for Rosalynn. How would she react if she knew the truth? "But this doesn't make Rosalynn a murderer. An opportunist, yes. By the way, Marco was out of town for training last week, so he's not the murderer either."

Max frowned. "How—"

"What about Mrs. Domenico?" Damien cut in. "Maybe she did it so her son could have the life insurance money?"

Lucy shook her head. "I don't think so. Mrs. Domenico can't guarantee that Rosalynn will say yes to the proposal. And with this kind of money, Rosalynn might want a prenuptial agreement. I know I would. It just seems too far-fetched to kill someone on the off chance that your son could indirectly benefit by marrying the widow."

"Rosalynn is still our prime suspect," Damien said. "Max is wiring me up, so I can listen in on the proposal."

Lucy gave Max a sideways glance. "What happened to the heist theory?"

Max blushed. "I never took the theory seriously. I was trying to throw you off the track because I don't want you involved in this investigation."

"Why? She's our secret weapon. I bet she found out about things we haven't even considered," Damien said. He turned to look at Lucy. "So, what did you find out?"

Lucy chewed her lower lip. She was willing to tell Max about Sander's secret, but she didn't want to do it in front of a reporter. But she was still a little miffed at the men for keeping their collaboration a secret.

Her cell phone chirped, saving her from the discussion. She pulled the phone out of her purse and paled at the message.

"What is it?" Damien asked.

"Is it your mom?" Max asked.

Lucy shook her head slowly. "It's from Tammy at the yarn shop. There's a fire at the PI office."

BY THE TIME Lucy and Stella arrived at the PI office, the firefighters were already putting out the last of the flames. Lucy parked on the side of the road. She didn't want to get in the way of the emergency vehicles in the parking lot. Tammy jogged over.

"Lucy!" Tammy said, giving Lucy a quick hug.

Lucy stiffened and forced herself to relax. She patted her friend's shoulder awkwardly. "Tell me what happened." She was proud that her voice didn't tremble. There was no need to panic yet. It might just be a minor fire. There might be minimal damage.

"I was restocking when I heard glass breaking outside. I ran out with my Glock"—Tammy waved the gun in front of Lucy's face, and Lucy took a step back—"but I didn't see anyone. And when I turned around to look inside the PI office, I saw the flames. I called nine-one-one lickety-split. And then I texted you. It must be a slow night because the fire truck got here in five minutes."

"You own a gun?" Stella asked.

"Ya-ah. What if some punk tries to rob me? I got

to be prepared," Tammy said. "I'm in the yarn shop by myself almost all the time. And I stay late sometimes to restock. Your internet ads are working, Lucy. I need to restock more often than usual."

"Why don't you put the gun away," Lucy said. "It might scare people with you waving that thing around."

"Good idea," Tammy said, tucking the gun into the waistband of her jeans. With her puffy jacket covering it, no one knew she was packing heat.

Lucy shivered. "We're lucky you stayed late tonight. If not, the entire shopping plaza could be up in flames." Even though she had insurance, it would still be months of headaches and paperwork before she even saw a cent of the insurance money. And in the meantime, she still had her mother's hospital bills. Whoever started the fire definitely knew how to hit where it hurt the most.

As the three women approached the shopping plaza, the scent of smoke and ashes grew stronger. Lucy blinked at the burning in her eyes. This was not the time for tears.

The fire chief and Max approached Lucy. She didn't see Damien in the parking lot, so he probably went to check on the newspaper office.

"Miss Fong," the fire chief said. "Most of the damage is in the front room. Luckily, the structure still looks sound, but you might want a contractor to come out and look at it. I would let it air out for a few more hours before going in to pick through the rubble."

Lucy swallowed, and when she spoke her voice came out in a croak. "How did the fire start?"

"Someone tossed a Molotov cocktail into the PI office," the fire chief said. "It will take a couple days for us to finish our report. You'll probably need it for your insurance."

Lucy nodded numbly. So the fire was intentional. Why would someone do this?

For the next half hour, Lucy worked on autopilot. The emergency officials left, leaving Lucy to secure the premises. Damien and Tammy tried to help, but Lucy waved them off. The fire crew had broken the rest of the large storefront windows to get inside.

Max put crime scene tape on the window, probably hoping to deter people from going inside. He said something, and Lucy nodded, but she could not recall what he actually said. He got into his police cruiser and left with Damien. Tammy locked up her shop and went home.

Lucy didn't even glance at the mess in the front room, locking the front door like it still mattered. By the time she dropped off Stella and went home, she was bone-weary and reeked of sweat and smoke. Her sinuses were so clogged, she couldn't even smell the clean ocean breeze that surrounded the Cape Cod house.

She sank to the floor of the kitchen with her back still pressed against the connecting garage door. The Little Emperor lifted his head from the water bowl and twitched his ears, watching her.

Lucy curled up, wrapping her arms around her knees. Why did someone want to burn down the PI office? They weren't actively investigating a case for a client. There was no incriminating evidence against anyone inside the building. The only case they were working on was Jason Albright's pro bono case, and very few people knew the Fayes were looking into it. How did it leak out?

Or maybe there wasn't a leak. Maybe Lucy had inadvertently alerted the murderer, and the fire was a diversion to keep Lucy busy and away from the investigation. The last two suspects on her list were Rosalynn Albright and Abby Frasier. But which woman was the murderer? Who had felt threatened enough to want Lucy off the case?

The Little Emperor padded over and sat next to her, his haunch brushing against her hip. Tears welled up in Lucy's eyes, and when she blinked, they tumbled out. She patted the cat, and for the first time, he purred as if to comfort her.

The PI business had been in the family for generations, and this was the second time the office had been violated. Maybe Lucy was in over her head. Unlike her mother, Lucy wasn't strong enough to shoulder the family business alone.

The next morning, Lucy went for a walk along the cliff, watching the rising sun splash fiery gold on the ocean. Across the bay, the circular lighthouse gained hues of yellow and orange on its white-washed stone wall. She breathed in the salty air, glad that her sinuses had cleared up overnight, and the tension drained from her shoulders. The events from the night before still whirled in a tangled mess in her mind, but it didn't feel as overwhelming this morning. There were still more questions than answers, which meant it was time to start putting the squeeze on folks.

Lucy came back inside the house, filled the food and water bowls for the Little Emperor. The Maine Coon was back to his former taciturn self, so he ignored her. At least something was normal this morning. She glanced at the clock in the kitchen. Just enough time for a quick visit with Mom and breakfast with Rosalynn.

When Lucy started her car, she noticed a note clipped to her windshield wiper. She blinked at it for half a second. Unless someone sneaked into the garage while she was out on the cliff, the note had probably been here since last night. She got out of the car and grabbed the note.

Printed on the white paper were bold capital letters:

STOP INVESTIGATING

Heat rose up in Lucy's chest, and a surge of anger ran through her. She crushed the paper and hurled it at the passenger seat. If the murderer had wanted to scare Lucy off, she should have stopped at the fire.

Lucy didn't kowtow to bullies, and this note was a bully trying to scare her off. This meant she was getting close, and this scared the murderer. Her lips twitched. It was time to see who had bigger nuggets —Lucy or the murderer.

19

KUNG FU

Lucy parked in the public parking lot across from the police station. She tapped on the recorder app on her phone and slipped it back into her purse. Someone had set the PI office on fire, and this person would have to pay.

As Lucy approached the Shoreline Bakery, she could see Rosalynn sitting at one of the outdoor bistro tables. Once again, her childhood friend was in a cable-knit sweater that did little to hide her muffin top. Her slim legs were in skinny jeans and black leather boots. Her helmet of glossy hair was no longer black but caramel with highlights.

Rosalynn waved enthusiastically, flashing the diamond on her finger. "Lucy, what do you want? My treat."

Lucy considered Rosalynn's offer for only a brief

second. It would be stupid to accept a coffee from a poisoner. "No, it's on me. To celebrate your engagement"

Rosalynn's jaw dropped. "How did you know?"

Lucy pointed at the ring. "You weren't wearing that the last time I saw you. Congratulations."

Rosalynn blushed. "No wonder you're a private investigator. You notice the details."

Lucy sank down into the chair next to Rosalynn and licked her lower lip. This was the perfect opening. "One of the workers saw you having lunch with Jason at the hospital cafeteria. Did you poison Jason's iced tea with antifreeze?"

Rosalynn stiffened, and she turned pale. "I... I didn't kill him."

"I didn't say you did. I just said you poisoned him."

Rosalynn's hands tightened around her purse straps. She opened and closed her mouth, but no words came out.

"Let me guess. You asked Jason out to lunch so he could sign the divorce papers, but he refused again. This is like your, what, fifth time asking him?"

"It was the sixth time," Rosalynn said in a tiny voice.

If Lucy hadn't been listening for it, she might have missed the comment entirely. She nodded. "You knew he wasn't going to give in or even make it easy for you. So you were angry, and you came prepared with a tiny bottle of antifreeze. Maybe you put it in a container no one would recognize. And when you went to get drinks at the fountain, you just slipped the antifreeze into his iced tea."

"I didn't want to kill him. I just wanted him to get sick. Like I get sick in the stomach every single time I have to deal with the jerk. I'm almost forty, childless, and living in a tiny apartment." Tears welled up in Rosalynn's eyes. "I just wanted to move on. But I couldn't." Her voice broke. "Because Jason refused to sign the divorce papers. There was always something to renegotiate. My life has been on hold for almost two years."

Lucy softened her voice. "How did you know he wouldn't die from the antifreeze?"

Rosalynn blotted her eyes with a tissue. "I did my research on the Internet."

"This is going to look real bad when it comes out. Not only are you getting Jason's life insurance policy, but you're marrying Marco almost imme-diately."

Rosalynn hiccupped. "I know. And now the police are probably after me. They're going to try to pin his death on me. But I didn't kill him. He was alive when I checked on him at the hospital."

Lucy straightened. "What time was this?"

"On the morning of his death. Right before the

ribbon-cutting ceremony at the children's wing with the mayor. I was on my coffee break."

Lucy gave her a deadpan stare. "That's when Jason died. Unless you have an alibi, you are in deep trouble."

"I was by myself. I didn't exactly want anyone to see me."

Lucy reached out and patted her friend's hand. "Get yourself a lawyer, and then enjoy the holidays. You look great, by the way. When did you get your hair done?"

Rosalynn patted her hair. "Last Thursday. They had a cancellation at the hair salon."

Lucy frowned. She had toured the Chinese Temple on Thursday. "What time was your appointment? Did you see Abby Frasier there?"

"It was about two o'clock." Rosalynn frowned, thinking. "I don't remember seeing Abby there. I was there for almost an hour. That was how busy they were. And I had the only cancellation."

"How did you find out about the cancellation?"

"The salon sent out an email to their newsletter subscribers, saying the first person to call gets the appointment. And I got it."

Lucy sank back into her chair. If Abby didn't get her hair done, then where was she that afternoon? Did she see Sander kiss the deputy mayor? Did she hear Sander confessing his secret to Stella and Lucy?

Her cell phone chirped. It was a list of names from Nurse Bobbi. These were the people she could identify from the photos taken during the ribbon-cutting ceremony at the hospital.

Lucy scanned through the names, looking for one name in particular. There! Toward the end of the list was Abby Frasier. She was at the scene of the crime on the day of the murder. She had to be the killer. Lucy's hand tightened on her phone.

"Is everything okay," Rosalynn asked.

Lucy dragged her gaze from the screen to study her former classmate. Could they become friends again? Probably not. Lucy couldn't forget how casually Rosalynn spoke of poisoning her husband. What if someday, Rosalynn got mad at Lucy and slipped something into her drink? No, Lucy would never be able to relax in Rosalynn's company ever again.

Lucy's cell phone chirped again. She tapped on the screen. The text message from Stella was sent ten minutes ago. The cell carrier had delayed the message.

SANDER WANTS TO TALK TO US AT HIS OFFICE. CAN YOU GET OVER THERE IN FIFTEEN MINUTES? I'M ALREADY ON MY WAY.

Lucy's gaze shifted across the street to the water

fountain and the Christmas tree in the middle of the square. A tall willowy woman with a pixie cut trotted up the steps of City Hall. Stella was already on her way to meet the mayor.

Why would the mayor want to meet them at City Hall on a weekend? It was quiet as a tomb. What if the message was from Abby? It would be easy enough for Abby to use Sander's phone to throw off Stella.

Lucy stood quickly, swaying as blood rushed to her head.

Rosalynn reached out to steady her. "Are you okay?"

Lucy pleaded with her friend. "Please call Max. I think Jason's killer just lured Stella to City Hall."

When Lucy glanced back at City Hall, Stella was nowhere in sight. Rosalynn looked hesitant. She probably didn't want anything to do with the police. Lucy didn't blame her, but this was a life-or-death situation.

As Lucy sprinted toward the town square, she called over her shoulder. "Hide your caller ID and talk to Max anonymously. We're counting on you to save us."

Lucy's heart beat painfully against her chest, and her shoulders were tight with tension. She had known fear before, but this time it was mixed with guilt. This was all her fault. She should have taken the time to explain the situation to Stella. Or at least emphasize that they shouldn't be alone with either of the Frasiers until the killer was caught. If anything happened to Stella, Lucy would never forgive herself.

The mist from the water fountain sprayed over Lucy's face, but it did little to cool her turbulent thoughts. Round the corner. Up the stairs. Her boots thudded against the stone steps. She yanked at the heavy mahogany door.

As Lucy ran across the marble floors, her steps echoed among the stone columns. At the bottom of the staircase, she paused for air. Her breaths came out in ragged puffs, and she clutched the railing for support. Some superhero. She could barely stand upright.

Lucy took a deep breath. As she climbed the flight of stairs to the second floor, her legs screamed. Jane Fonda had not done a good job in preparing Lucy for this moment. She paused at the top of the landing for another breather. She hurried to the mayor's door.

Two shadows could be seen in the frosted glass insert on the door. Someone chuckled.

Lucy paused, assessing the situation. Was that an evil laugh or a friendly one? She tightened the grip on her purse strap and grabbed the doorknob. She ran in, screaming like a banshee and swinging her purse in front of her like it was a nunchuck.

"Back off! I know kung fu!" Lucy screamed.

Sander and Stella leaped back, holding up both hands, palms out.

"Whoa!" Sander said.

"What did you drink this morning?" Stella asked.

Lucy froze, scanning the reception room. Empty plush leather sofa. No one at the mahogany desk. Where was Abby? Unless she was under the desk, there was no other place to hide.

Lucy closed her eyes, wishing for a wormhole. Anything that would let her break the time-space continuum so she could have a do-over. Heat rose from her chest and traveled up to her neck. Her face felt like a too-tight balloon. This was not a trap to get rid of Stella. It was a legitimate business meeting with the mayor. And Lucy had just proven she was a lunatic.

Lucy opened her eyes and gave Sander a weak smile. "Sorry about that." She did a fist pump. "I am just so excited to have this meeting to discuss the museum lease." She closed the door quietly behind her. She was a professional.

Sander gave Stella a sideways glance. He didn't believe Lucy for one moment. "Calla Louie's organization is suing the town over the Monkey King artifact. Until this lawsuit is resolved, there will be no museum."

Lucy cut her eyes to Stella, who shrugged. "But what about the other exhibits?"

"The tourists can see railroad equipment elsewhere. It's not a big enough draw. We will lose money leasing a temporary location. But don't worry. We will continue to fundraise for a permanent museum."

Lucy sighed. This was political speak for no project until they get more funding.

Bam!

The door banged open behind them. Lucy almost jumped out of her skin. She swung around with her heart in her throat.

Max and Officer Martinez came into the room with their guns drawn. "Hands in the air," Max shouted.

Three sets of hands went up into the air.

Lucy's face got even hotter. Holy Toledo! How was she going to explain this? She gave the officers a weak smile. "It's a false alarm. I'm sorry."

Max narrowed his eyes and lowered his gun. Officer Martinez followed suit.

"What is going on here?" Sander thundered.

Max gave Lucy a pointed look. "We got an anonymous tip that Jason's killer got Stella."

All four sets of eyes turned to stare at Lucy.

"What's up with this anonymous tip? Why is it always anonymous?" Lucy mused out loud, staring at the ceiling and avoiding eye contact. Yep, she was a real professional, all right.

Max and Officer Martinez bid their goodbyes and left. Apparently, they didn't want to get into a philosophical discussion about anonymous callers.

"I think we are done here," Sander said. He sounded like he regretted asking for this meeting, and Lucy didn't blame him.

Lucy backed out of the room. "Oookay. Have a good weekend." She glanced at Stella.

"We will finish up our chat," Stella said.

Sander opened the inner door to his office. If Lucy hadn't known better, she might have suspected the two of them were having an affair. But as it was, they were just close childhood friends that grew up to be close adult friends.

Lucy left the room and closed the door softly behind her. Now that was an embarrassing meeting. She didn't even know how to explain herself the next time she met up with Max. Or maybe she didn't have to say anything. After all, she didn't make that anonymous phone call. Rosalynn had her own problems, so she might not rat Lucy out.

As her boots thudded on the tile floor, Lucy considered her next move. Max would need to know what she had found out in her investigation. He would need to follow up with the FBI. While Lucy felt bad for Sander, it was still wrong to hire an assassin—even in an insomniac fit of anger. It was above her pay grade to figure out how to deal with it, but she couldn't ignore it. And then she would need to have a serious talk with Stella about avoiding the Frasiers until the police arrested Abby.

At the top of the landing for the staircase, the hair on the back of Lucy's neck stiffened. She paused, straining her ears. What was that? She glanced over her shoulder to see Abby looking right back at her.

20

FINALLY HOME

Lucy's eyes widened, and her hands tightened on her purse strap. She reached into her jacket pocket and pulled out a key ring. The keys for the vacant shop. She certainly had weapons of mass destruction.

Abby stepped around the column as if she had been waiting for Lucy. She approached slowly. Her soft moccasins didn't make any sound on the tile floor. The tan trench coat swished each time she moved. With the ceiling light behind her, Abby's face was hidden in the shadows.

Lucy's leg muscles tensed for flight. Even though the mayor's wife hadn't said a word nor had she done anything to threaten Lucy, a warning bell clamored in the back of her head. The sight of Abby's gloved hands sent a shiver down Lucy's back. The black leather wouldn't leave behind fingerprints.

Even if Lucy screamed, Sander and Stella couldn't hear her. They were too far away and behind closed doors. And Max and Officer Martinez had left the building a while ago. Lucy was alone with Jason's killer at the top of a staircase.

She took a step back. Maybe she could jump on the railing and slide all the way down like they did in the movies. Or maybe she could still pretend to be ignorant of Abby's crime.

Lucy forced a smile on her face. "Oh, hi Abby. I can't chat. I need to get back to the office. I have a client coming in, wanting me to overhaul their website." There. She was a marketing consultant, not a PI.

"I saw you and Stella snooping around my house." Abby took a step closer. "The two of you have been busy little beavers, poking your nose in other people's business."

Lucy took another step back. She glanced over her shoulder quickly. One more step, and she would be at the edge of the landing. "I... I don't know what you're talking about. We were discussing the museum lease with Sander."

"That evening, Sander asked me for a divorce."

"What? Why?" Lucy asked. Fabulous. Abby would undoubtedly blame Lucy for this as well.

"When it was just Jason, I was able to convince Sander to let me deal with it. But once you and Stella knew about Sander's preference, he figured there was no point in pretending to be a happy family. It was never a pretense for me." Abby's voice cracked at the end.

Lucy shivered again. That crack held a whole ocean of hurt, and it was directed at her. She had to keep Abby talking. As long as she was moving her lips, she wasn't trying to strangle Lucy. And maybe Sander and Stella would come out of the office and see them.

"I don't get it," Lucy said, hoping she sounded like a concerned friend. "Why do you want to stay married to Sander? Isn't it better to be alone than miserable in a marriage?"

"I wasn't miserable," Abby said with sincerity. "I had everything. I live in a big house. And my son is expecting his first child. And as the mayor's wife, I get invited to all the committees. All those stuck-up women who used to turn their noses up at me as a child now have to kiss up to me. I have come a long way from sleeping on a sofa bed with my siblings in a trailer. I am a success. Why would I want to change any of that?"

"Sander said he didn't know Jason got hired by the city. That was your doing, wasn't it?"

"Jason was a con man who knew which way the

wind blew. When he couldn't get anything out of Sander, he approached me. Yes, I got him the job, and I told him about the Monkey King artifact."

"I'm surprised he didn't ask you to steal it for him," Lucy said.

"He asked, and I kept putting him off. I knew he wouldn't stop bothering us. He wouldn't stop bothering me. So when I saw him lying in the hospital bed, it was all too easy to just take care of him." Abby flexed her fingers.

Lucy's mouth went dry. It all made sense now. "You were at the ribbon-cutting ceremony at the hospital with Sander. All eyes were on him, so you slipped away unnoticed."

Abby stepped into the light. She raised an eyebrow at Lucy, a half-smile on her face. "No one is coming. Sander and Stella took the side entrance. It's a shorter distance to the parking lot, and Sander likes to take shortcuts."

She rushed at Lucy, her gloved hands outstretched.

Lucy took a side step just like Jane Fonda showed her in the exercise video, flinging her arms up in the air. Her right arm connected with Abby's shoulder. It was a light tap, but it was enough to put the mayor's wife off balance.

For half a heartbeat, Abby wobbled on the edge of the landing, and she began to tumble. Down,

down, she went. Head over heels. Thumping against the stone steps. Her trench coat swishing all the way down.

Lucy stared wide-eyed in horror. With trembling hands, she pulled out her cell phone and called nine-one-one. When she hung up, she noticed the recording app had been on since her conversation with Rosalynn at the bakery. She had an audio file of Abby's confession.

"Hi, Mom. It's Lucy again. If you can hear me, please move your fingers." She paused, waiting for movement.

The medical machines whirred, and the clock ticked. But nothing from her mom.

Of course, there was nothing. Why did she expect it to be different this time?

Lucy took a deep breath, shaking off her worry. She would not stress about this. It was beyond her control.

It had been a week since Abby's arrest. Lucy had been too busy providing police statements, dealing with insurance, getting contractor quotes, and meeting new clients. Faye Investigations finally had their first client under the new management.

Her morning visits to Mom became shorter and

shorter. Just a quick peek. She had actually skipped the last two mornings.

But now, it was the weekend, and Lucy had plenty of time this morning. As she talked about the murder investigation, she held her mother's hand.

"I don't know what I'm doing, but I seem to be doing all right. Don't worry, Mom. I'll keep the business going until you wake up. I won't let you down."

Footsteps approached her mother's hospital room. Lucy glanced at the door. Maybe it was Nurse Bobbi.

Damien appeared in the doorway, holding two cups of coffee from the Shoreline Bakery. He handed her one and leaned against the doorframe. The room was small, but it suddenly felt even smaller, like he sucked all the air out of the room.

Lucy sipped the coffee, inhaling the nutty aromatic flavor. She was still irritated with him for keeping her in the dark. And the fact that she cared had her worried. She wasn't ready to be involved with anyone.

"Why do I have Jason Albright's therapy chicken in my printer shed?" he asked. "And what am I supposed to do with the eggs?"

"The chicken is a hen? If you don't want the eggs, give them to me. I can boil them for breakfast," Lucy said.

"I'm assuming you're giving the chicken food and

water." Damien raised an eyebrow. "Are you cleaning up after the chicken poop as well?"

"Hey, that's your problem. Maybe you should lock your shed, then you wouldn't find a bottle of antifreeze in it."

"Touché."

"I thought I was helping a friend, but instead, I was a chump."

"I'm sorry," Damien said. "When Max brought me in for questioning over the antifreeze, I was anxious. So, when he proposed a partnership between us, what else could I say, but yes? At the time, I didn't know how Jason Albright died. Max thought I could get the locals to talk to me." Damien chuckled. "I guess now we know who the locals will talk to."

Lucy harrumphed and took another sip of coffee. "If you keep the chicken a while longer, then we are square. I can't bring her home yet. I need to build a coop that can keep out a cat."

"You got yourself a deal. By the way, I need your help again."

Lucy got up and thrust the coffee cup back at his face. "Take this back. I don't want to have anything to do with this or your schemes."

Damien took a step back. "It's not what you think. I want to hire you for some PR work."

Lucy sank back into her chair. "Okay, I'm listening." She took a sip of coffee.

"I'm running for mayor," Damien said.

Lucy choked, snorting coffee out of her nose. The brown liquid splattered over her lilac sweater.

Damien dug into his jeans pocket, pulled out a crumpled napkin, and held it out to her. "That was some reaction."

Lucy grabbed the napkin and blotted her sweater. "What do you need from me?"

Damien gave her a wide grin like it was her lucky day. "I was hoping you would become my campaign manager."

Lucy's heart sank. No way. "Let me think about it."

After a few more minutes of chitchat, Damien left, leaving Lucy alone with her thoughts and her mom.

"I can't believe Damien wants to be mayor," Lucy said out loud.

"Anyone but Damien," a tiny voice croaked.

Lucy stiffened and froze. Her wide eyes swiveled to her mother's form on the hospital bed. "Mama?"

Mom's eyes opened to half-mast, but they were looking straight back at Lucy. She licked her lower lip. "Hi, baby. Mama's back."

Lucy's eyes filled with tears, and she had to clear

her throat several times before she could speak. "Me, too, Mama. I'm home."

Meet Raina Sun
Raining Men and Corpses
(Raina Sun #1)
free ebook

Meet Cedar Woods
Arrest the Allies
(Cedar Woods Mystery #1)

Get Anne R. Tan's FREE Starter Library at http://annertan.com/newsletter

ACKNOWLEDGMENTS

A story is a dream that a writer brings to life on paper. But a book needs a team to nurture it into the enjoyable tale you've just read.

I want to thank my editors, Alicia S. and Brandee, for wrangling my words so they are coherent.

And then, there are my wonderful beta-readers—Joyce S., Cindy I., Della D., Susan J., and Debi P.—thank you, ladies, for volunteering your time to catch these sneaky typos and grammatical errors.

And finally, thank you, Susan C. for the awesome cover.

I wouldn't have been able to bring this story to life without all of you, wonderful ladies. Thank you!

—Anne R. Tan

ALSO BY ANNE R. TAN

Thanks for reading *Just A Lucky Break-In*. I hope you enjoyed it!

Did you like this book?

Please review my books at your favorite book retailer. As an indie author, reviews help other readers find my books. I appreciate all reviews, whether positive or negative.

Want to know about new releases, sale pricing, and exclusive content?

Sign up for Anne R. Tan's email newsletter at http://annertan.com/newsletter

Your information would not be sold or transferred. Thank you for trusting me with your email.

Want More Lucy Fong?

Just Shoot Me Dead (Lucy Fong #1)

Just Lost and Found (Lucy Fong #1.5)

Just a Lucky Break-In (Lucy Fong #2)

How about another series by Anne R. Tan?

Raining Men and Corpses (Raina Sun #1) - Free

Gusty Lovers and Cadavers (Raina Sun #2)

Breezy Friends and Bodies (Raina Sun #3)

Balmy Darlings and Death (Raina Sun #4)

Sunny Mates and Murders (Raina Sun #5)

Murky Passions and Scandals (Raina Sun #6)

Smoldering Flames and Secrets (Raina Sun #7)

Hazy Grooms and Homicides (Raina Sun #8)

Chilly Comforts and Disasters (Raina Sun #9)

Fair Cronies and Felonies (Raina Sun #10)

Airy Allies and Enemies (Raina Sun #11)

RAINING MEN AND CORPSES

Raina Sun studied her flushed face in the mirror of the restroom, hoping for an attack of diarrhea or food poisoning. Anything to delay the upcoming confrontation with her graduate advisor. She pulled her shirt away from her body and sniffed. No B.O. Just the industrial strength Pine-Sol and cloying lemon cleanser the janitor had used to clean the place.

She splashed water on her face and toweled it off. The trek from the bus stop to the history building in this August heat had turned her curly black hair into a fuzz ball. A Chinese girl with an Afro. Not exactly the image of a ballbuster.

While Raina would eventually recover from being a fool in love, she wasn't willing to lose two thousand dollars to learn this lesson. Not when she had lawyer's fees gobbling up her savings and bald tires giving her heart palpitations every time she got behind the wheel.

For the first time, Raina wished she was more physically commanding. With her petite frame, she wasn't a real threat to anything larger than a pygmy goat. But it was time to up the ante and to pester Holden Merritt like a fly on a fresh pile of crap. She wasn't walking out of this meeting empty-handed.

Taking a deep breath to calm her fluttering stomach, Raina banged open the restroom door in a show of bravado that echoed through the hall. A paunchy student glanced in her direction but returned to his study of the bulletin boards. Raina stalked into her graduate advisor's office, preparing to do battle. She was all woman. She was a lioness. She was courageous. The cheesy affirmations became a prayer for strength.

Holden continued scribbling on his yellow legal pad and gestured for her to have a seat. "Let me finish this thought." He chewed on his pencil and wrote a couple more sentences.

Raina dropped onto the chair in front of his desk and folded her arms across her chest. So much for ruffling his feathers. The scratching of the pencil and the ticking clock tightened the knot in her stomach. She shifted in the chair, wondering how she should bring up the loan. Her upbringing had made discussing money taboo, and even as an adult, she had trouble talking about it.

Just ask for the money back, said a small voice in her head.

Her skin itched at the neatness in his office. On the shelves lining one wall, books were alphabetized by subject and authors' last names. No crammed volumes in the space above the shelved books like in her apartment. On the opposite wall, framed covers of his published books hung in neat lines, forming a perfect grid. As in previous visits, she resisted the urge to nudge a frame by a small degree just to see how long it would take for him to notice.

A place for everything and everything in its place, just like the blond man with the crisp collared shirt sitting in front of her. The pale light filtering in from the dusty windows behind Holden gave him a tarnished halo. He was a tall man with strong shoulders and a confident aura. She had once found his heavy-lidded brown eyes mesmerizing. Now he just looked tired, but he was still spit-and-polished within an inch of his life.

Holden placed the pencil on the center of the pad and folded his hands on the desk. "Have you decided which countries you want to focus on?"

Raina unclenched the fists resting on her lap. So he was going to pretend they were nothing more than a professor and grad student. "China and Japan look to be a good option."

"Good choice. Unfortunately, you'll need to take beginning language classes with the undergrads. It's too bad classes from your undergrad engineering degree don't apply towards your graduate degree." He turned to open the low filing cabinet underneath the window and pulled out several sheets of paper. "We need to declare your area of focus before the end of the semester."

Raina scowled at his back. If he wanted to pretend nothing had happened between them over the summer, she could do the same...after she got her money back. She smoothed her face and tugged at her earlobe. "My car is having problems. When can you pay me back?" Great. She sounded like a pansy.

Holden flashed a commercial-worthy smile. "Sorry, I don't get paid until the end of next week." He scribbled on the margin of the top page of the pile and pushed the stack toward her. "Here's the information for this semester."

Raina took a deep breath. She couldn't believe this. He made it sound like she was asking him for a favor. "That's what you said last time. Why don't you post-date a check for me? I'll deposit it next week."

"Sorry, I don't have my checkbook with me."

Her forced smile became brittle. "Why don't you

log in online and post-date a bank check? I can wait."

He tapped his pencil on the desk. "Look, I don't have time—"

Raina sagged against the chair. "I need the money. I'm late—" The knot in her chest tightened until it strangled her voice. He wouldn't care about her late bills. This angle wouldn't appeal to a selfish person.

Holden licked his lips. He gave her a wobbly and hopeful smile. "I...I don't know what to say. Are you sure?"

Raina nodded, not trusting her voice. There was something in his voice. Was he listening to her for the first time? She cleared her throat and opened her mouth. To do what? Threaten to expose their affair? She closed her mouth, waiting for his next move.

They stared at each other, and the clock leisurely swallowed the minutes and filled the silence between them.

"The money?" Raina finally whispered.

Heels clicked on the hallway floor, and someone knocked on the open door.

Holden jerked up like a tangled puppet, and his chair scuffed against the floor. He grabbed the pile of papers in front of him and knocked over the mahogany pencil caddy Raina had given him for his birthday.

Raina glanced behind her.

Gail, the history department's secretary, stood at the door. Her thick brows were a tight line across her forehead. "Sorry to interrupt. Holden, you're late for the meeting with the Dean. He's in the conference room."

Holden squeezed Raina's shoulder as he stepped around his desk. "Let's talk later," he whispered.

The fluttering returned to Raina's stomach. She resisted the urge to brush the feel of his hand from her shoulder.

"Are you okay, hon?" Gail asked.

"Yes. I..." Raina nodded. "Yes, thank you."

"Just let me know if I can help." Gail left the room and the sound of her clicking heels faded in the hall.

Raina took a couple of deep breaths, staring at the tiny window in front of her. Holden's reaction was strange. What was up with that strange smile? He looked as if Raina had given him a gift...

Her eyes widened. Wait! Did he think she was late late? Did he think she was pregnant? Her gut twisted at the thought. Why should she feel guilty about wanting her money back? It wasn't her fault he jumped to the wrong conclusion.

Her eyes flicked to the knocked-over pencils and the small framed photograph next to them. She turned the frame around, and her eyes widened in surprise at the blonde. New girlfriend already? He sure got over her fast enough. She replaced the picture frame face down on the desk. Yes, it was petty, but she'd never claimed to be gracious.

Raina left the office and trudged toward the computer labs for her shift. She didn't expect Holden to pay up with a smile, but now things were even more complicated. Tomorrow's fundraiser committee meeting would be awkward with a fake pregnancy hanging between them. Awkwardness she could power through, but her lawyer wasn't going to work for an IOU.

The sky was turning pink when she drove home through the downtown area. Most of the mom-and-pop shops were closed, but there were still people frolicking in Hook Park, enjoying the delta breeze after another hot, record-breaking day. The strands of lights in the outdoor seating areas and the few bicycles rolling next to parked cars were part of the charm that made Raina seek refuge in the small town of Gold Springs. Far enough away from her family in San Francisco, where the two-hour drive was a convenient excuse to skip out on birthday parties and last minute family gatherings.

At the corner of Second and B Street, Raina

slowed and squinted at the bank's parking lot. Was that Holden? Two heavyset men in dark suits with bored expressions held Holden by the elbows between them. Holden's wide eyes had the trapped appearance of an animal in a cage. The three of them got into a shiny black SUV with chrome spinners.

The car behind her honked, and Raina drove through the intersection. By the time she circled the block, the black car was gone. The two well-dressed men had to be thugs, and apparently they worked for someone who cared about appearances.

Should she call the police? But what would she tell them? Her ex-boyfriend got into a car with two big men? She shook her head. This was none of her business. She needed to focus on getting her money back and clearing the air with Holden. It had crossed her mind to let him continue to believe she was pregnant, but this was plain stupid. She didn't want to come off as a vindictive girl using a preg-nancy lie to get back at a man.

Raina drove home on autopilot. She lived in a small complex on the edge of the downtown area, which consisted of two strips of four units facing each other like the little green houses on a Monopoly game. She threw her purse on the narrow side table and turned on the lamp next to her olive-colored sofa. The soft glow filled the living room and cast shadows into the breakfast nook. She glanced around the space with pride. Her apartment might be small, but it was bigger than the attic bedroom in San Francisco. And it was all hers.

Above the TV, the clock with gilded koi fishes swimming around the dial said it was past dinnertime. And because Raina was no longer on someone else's dinner schedule—her mother insisted on dinner at five thirty—she didn't have to eat until she felt like it. Even after a year of being on her own for the first time, it still felt great.

Raina flopped down on the new-to-me sofa, shifting on the thick cushions, and picked up the book on the floor. She was immersed in the world of Middle Earth when there was a sharp knock on her front door. Cocking her head, she waited, in case it was the dressed-up church people trying to convince her to give up her Sunday mornings. The knock came again. She glanced at the gap between the curtains of the closed window above her sofa. No church person, but she wasn't sure an inquisitive reporter was much of an improvement.

Eden Small, her friend and neighbor, hunched and squinted at the peephole like she thought Raina was watching her. She worked for the *Gold Springs Weekly*, the town's newspaper and sometimes entertainment rag. Eden wasn't the type to let a closed door stop her. With one hand holding a pizza box, she whipped out her cell phone and tapped on it.

When the phone in the kitchen rang, Raina laughed. Her friend wasn't someone who took no for an answer. Raina tossed the book on the sofa and opened the front door to look up, up, and up.

Even without her three-inch heels, Eden towered over Raina by a good seven inches. Her deep brown skin shone with health and vitality. Before Raina could utter a greeting, Eden shoved the pizza box into Raina's hands. "I forgot my soda."

Her graceful friend turned, and her silky brown weave fanned out like a shampoo commercial, glittering in the dim light. The scent of lavender lingered in the air even after she hustled across the courtyard toward her apartment.

Raina left the door open and dropped the pizza box on the square Goodwill dining room table. She filled a glass of water for herself and grabbed some napkins.

Eden returned with a can of soda and locked the front door. "Did you get your money back?"

Raina told her friend everything that had happened on campus and the strange incident at the bank. "I haven't seen Holden in two months, but he seemed diminished today. A little less larger than life."

"It's called taking off the rose-colored glasses,"

Eden said. "I can't believe he jumped straight to the pregnancy idea. I'm surprised he didn't shove a check into your hands to get rid of you."

"I'm not quite sure what to make of it. It almost sounded like Holden wanted to be a father."

"He's playing mind games with you."

Raina grimaced. Her friend was probably right. "Back in June, you should have snatched those glasses from me and smacked my nose with them."

Eden rolled her eyes. "As if you would have listened."

Raina ignored the comment. Her friend was probably right about this one too. "So when is Phil supposed to pick his EIC trainee?"

"Assistant Editor-in-Chief. Not trainee. Unofficially, the position is supposed to be his replacement when he retires. I need a story that'll make me stand out. I'm thinking about resurrecting an old gossip"—Eden gave her a sideways glance—"about Holden and Olivia."

Raina played with the cheese on her pizza. Did she want to get involved in this? A smart woman would probably change the subject. "I'll bite. What is the rumor?"

"This has nothing to do with you. It's perfect timing with the upcoming annual Christmas fundraiser."

"Got it! It's not about me. What's the rumor?"

"The history department got a huge grant. It was supposed to be divided among the other professors, but Holden got fifty percent." Eden wiggled her eyebrows. "He spent far too much time in the boss's office to be strictly professional."

"Olivia Kline is old enough to be his mother!"

"I'm just repeating what the wagging tongues said."

Raina flushed, and she shifted her gaze to the pizza on her plate. So Holden cheated on her while they were together?

"This was before you came on the scene," Eden added quickly. "But that's not the interesting part." She paused. "Another twenty percent of the grant money grew legs."

"What makes you think Holden has anything to do with the missing money?"

Eden shrugged. "But wouldn't it be juicy if he did?"

Raina didn't reply. This sounded more like gossip mongering than news, but wasn't there a grain of truth in every story?

After Eden left, Raina sorted her mail. On top of the pile of junk mail was a cream-colored envelope from her lawyer. Apparently, another cousin had decided to join the suit contesting the inheritance from her grandfather. At the rate things were going, the lawyer fees would swallow the entire three million dollars. Her grandfather didn't do Raina any favor by asking her to forward the money to his secret second family in China. Once again, being the good girl had backfired on her.

She took a deep breath. One thing at a time. First, Holden. Then, her family.

Raining Men and Corpses
(Raina Sun #1)
Available now.

ABOUT THE AUTHOR

Anne R. Tan is a *USA Today* bestselling author. She writes the Raina Sun Mystery series and the Lucy Fong Mystery series. Her humorous cozy mysteries feature Chinese-American amateur sleuths dealing with love, family, and life while solving murders.

Sign up for her newsletter for new release announcement, sales, and exclusive content at http://annertan.com/newsletter/